Let's all draw
MONSTERS
ghosts, ghouls and demons

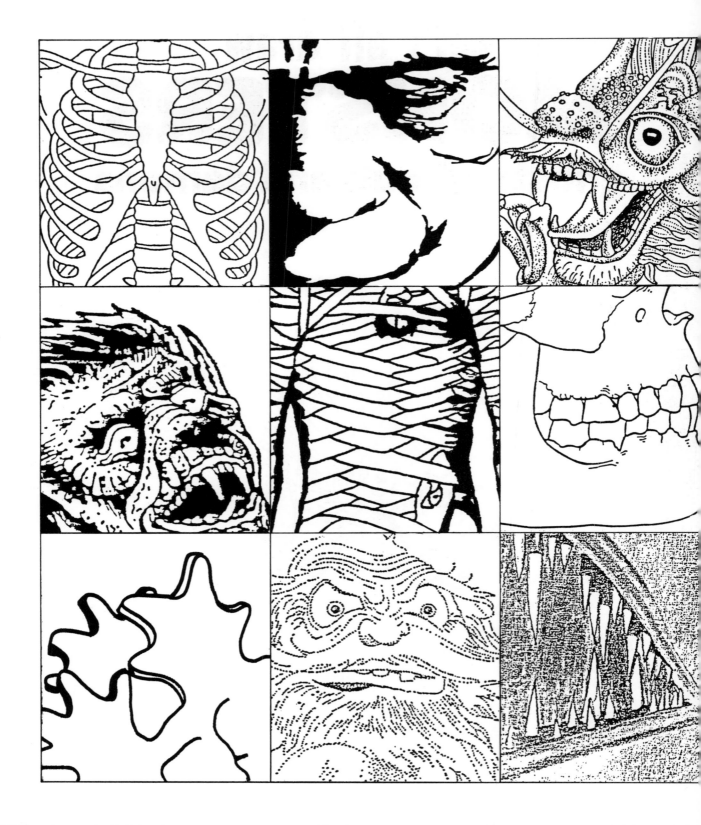

Here and at the back of the book are details
from some of the drawings featured. Can
you find the pages on which they appear?

Also in this series:

LET'S ALL DRAW CARS
trucks and other vehicles

LET'S ALL DRAW CATS
dogs and other animals

LET'S ALL DRAW DINOSAURS
pterodactyls and other prehistoric creatures

Illustrations by
Darren Bennett, James Dallas, Ryozo Kohira,
Paul McCauley, Kathleen McDougall, Bruce Robertson,
Jane Robertson, Michael Robertson, Graham Rosewarne,
Tim Scrivens, Dino Skeete

© Diagram Visual Information Ltd 1990

First published in 1991 in the United States by Watson-Guptill Publications, a division of BPI Communications, Inc., 1515 Broadway, New York, New York 10036.

Library of Congress Cataloging-in-Publication Data

Robertson, Jane, 1965–
  Let's all draw monsters, ghosts, ghouls, and demons/Jane Robertson; text by Sue Pinkus.
    p.   cm. – (Let's all draw)
  Summary: Provides step-by-step instructions for drawing a variety of monsters, including vampires, aliens, skeletons, and specific favorites such as King Kong and Godzilla.
  ISBN 0-8230-2707-4
  1. Monsters in art – Juvenile literature. 2. Drawing – Technique – Juvenile literature. [1. Monsters in art. 2. Drawing – Technique.] I. Pinkus, Sue. II. Title. III. Series.
NC825. M6R6 1991
743 – dc20   90-40281
                                                    CIP
                                                    AC

Typeset by Bournetype, Bournemouth, England
Printed and bound by Snoeck Ducaju & Sons, Ghent, Belgium

1 2 3 4 5 / 96 95 94 93 92 91

Let's all draw
MONSTERS
ghosts, ghouls and demons

JANE ROBERTSON

Text by Sue Pinkus

WATSON-GUPTILL PUBLICATIONS/NEW YORK

About this book

Like lots of people, you probably enjoy being just a bit frightened at times. This book will show you how to draw all sorts of crazy monsters to scare yourself and also terrify your friends.

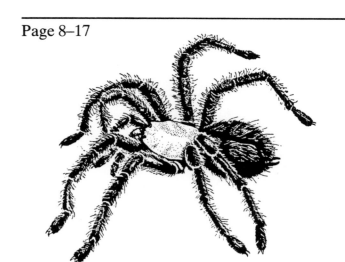

WHAT IS A MONSTER?

First, in **Part 1**, take a look at some of the strangest creatures you could possibly dream up. Of course, they don't really exist, but have been created by artists or writers. You may have seen monsters like these in cartoons on TV, in comics and books, or as toys and models. Most are very scary. Some have just one or even three eyes, or wings; others are even weirder. Watch out! There's a monster about!

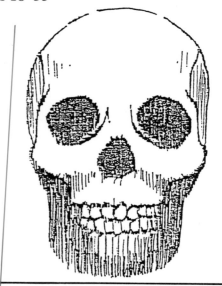

GETTING READY TO DRAW

In **Part 2**, find out all you need to know about using pencils, felt-tips, ballpoint pens, brushes, paints, chalks and other tools so you can begin to draw monsters like a true artist.

Pick up a pencil! You'll soon be drawing some of the scariest pictures you can imagine. There are some great ideas for things to do with your drawings when you have finished them, too.

As you can see, this book has large page numbers. They are there to help you find your way easily to a drawing you might need to look at again while you are working.

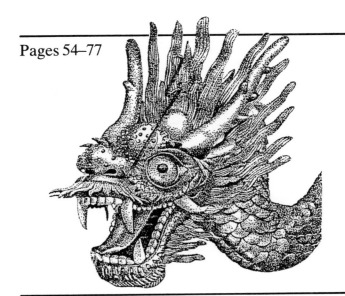

DRAWING MONSTERS' HEADS

Part 3 explores the way you can start to draw amazingly terrifying pictures of heads of all kinds – dragons and witches among them.

YOUR MONSTER HORROR SHOW

In **Part 4**, there's a whole horror show of monsters for you to look at and copy, and there are lots of expert hints and special tips as well. You'll soon be on your way to making some fantastic drawings of monsters, never fear!

Part 1

This ferocious dragon with its long tail, sharp teeth, spiky claws and beard is a legendary monster often found in ancient Chinese stories. (Perhaps you have seen the dragon dance that is performed by Chinese people all over the world on their New Year's Day.) Dragons do not actually exist, but they are usually shown with green bodies covered in scales, and they sometimes have wings.

There are, of course, many other monsters – vampires, giants and werewolves, for instance – and quite a few famous ones, like King Kong, are featured in books and films. But there are also strange, smaller creatures that are said only to come out at night when you are fast asleep – goblins, trolls and dwarfs, for example.

What makes you scared?

People are scared of all sorts of different things – mice, gorillas, large snakes, spiders or ghosts. Is there something that would make you scream or freeze to the spot?

Perhaps you have a bad dream sometimes. I know I do. An angry giant is chasing me, and is just about to catch up with me when, fortunately, I wake up.

The creature opposite is a dryad. The smaller drawing looks just like an ordinary tree in the woods, but sometimes it turns into a terrifying monster. Next time you are out and about, see if you can spot one - unless, of course, you don't believe they exist.

When you were smaller, did you sometimes feel scared of the dark? You knew there was nothing there, but still you felt frightened and hid under the covers because you thought there might be a monster like this giant spider under the bed or behind the wardrobe. Really, it was all in your imagination.

Legendary monsters

Ever since ancient times, writers have imagined the most fantastic creatures and woven them into wonderful stories, describing them in great detail. Cerberus, for instance, was the huge three-headed dog shown here, who guarded the entrance to the Underworld in Greek mythology. (Some say he had 50 heads. They would take a very long time to draw, but you can try if you like.) The only way to stop him from snarling was to offer him cake, so the legend goes. But one man, Orpheus, sent him to sleep by playing sweet music on an instrument called a lyre.

Whenever there is a full moon, some people are said to turn into werewolves. You may not believe this legend, but you can still have fun copying the series of drawings shown here. (When is the next full moon? Make sure you are safely home, or beware!) Find out more about how to draw them on Pages 30–31 and 92.

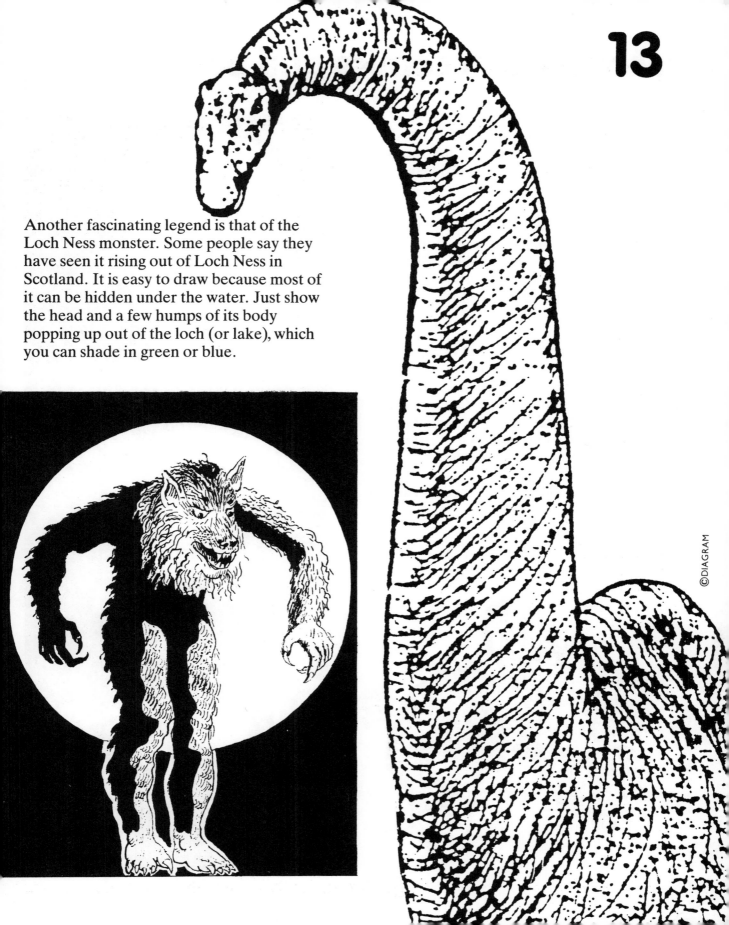

Another fascinating legend is that of the
Loch Ness monster. Some people say they
have seen it rising out of Loch Ness in
Scotland. It is easy to draw because most of
it can be hidden under the water. Just show
the head and a few humps of its body
popping up out of the loch (or lake), which
you can shade in green or blue.

©DIAGRAM

Monsters in comics and books

Many people have written or illustrated famous books full of spine-chilling monsters and weird creatures that will thrill your imagination.

Have you ever read *Gulliver's Travels* by Jonathan Swift? In this famous story, Gulliver has lots of remarkable adventures when he meets a race of giants (the Brobdingnagians) and some little people, too.

Perhaps you know the stories of *Alice in Wonderland* (known as *Alice's Adventures Underground* in the United States) and also *Alice Through the Looking Glass* by Lewis Carroll. Alice once became so small when she drank a magic potion that everything around her suddenly seemed huge.

In this illustration shown below, we can see her meeting a talking dodo.

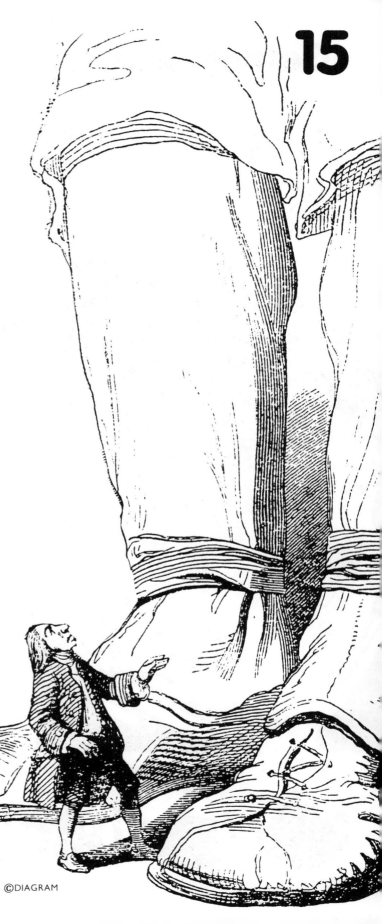

The idea for Frankenstein's monster, above, in Mary Shelley's story came to her in a nightmare. A monster is created by a doctor and starts to haunt the district, committing several murders. Turn to pages 62–63 and 86–87 for other pictures of this violent creature.

There are lots of other stories about terrifying beings, too. If you find some in books or comics, you might like to try to draw them.

This is not a midget. It's Gulliver with a giant known as a Brobdingnagian.

©DIAGRAM

Getting ideas

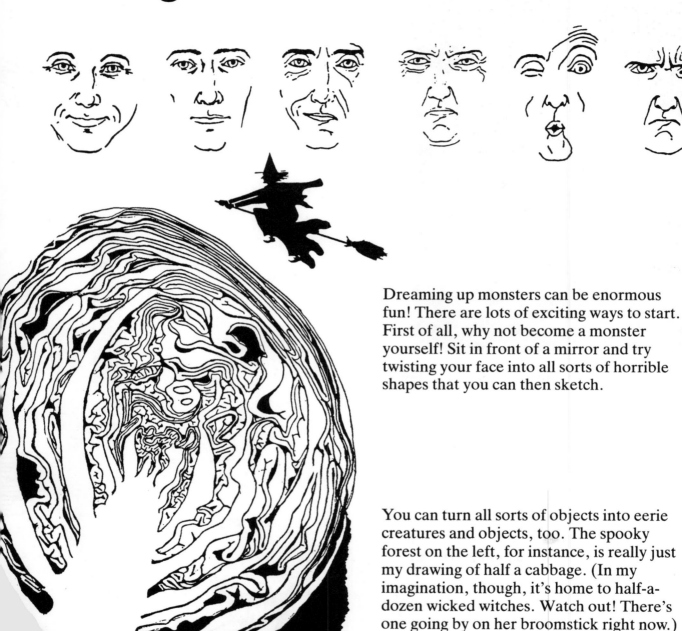

Dreaming up monsters can be enormous fun! There are lots of exciting ways to start. First of all, why not become a monster yourself! Sit in front of a mirror and try twisting your face into all sorts of horrible shapes that you can then sketch.

You can turn all sorts of objects into eerie creatures and objects, too. The spooky forest on the left, for instance, is really just my drawing of half a cabbage. (In my imagination, though, it's home to half-a-dozen wicked witches. Watch out! There's one going by on her broomstick right now.)

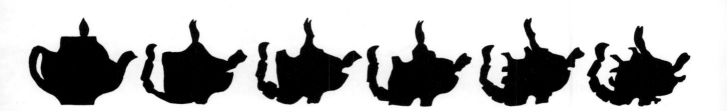

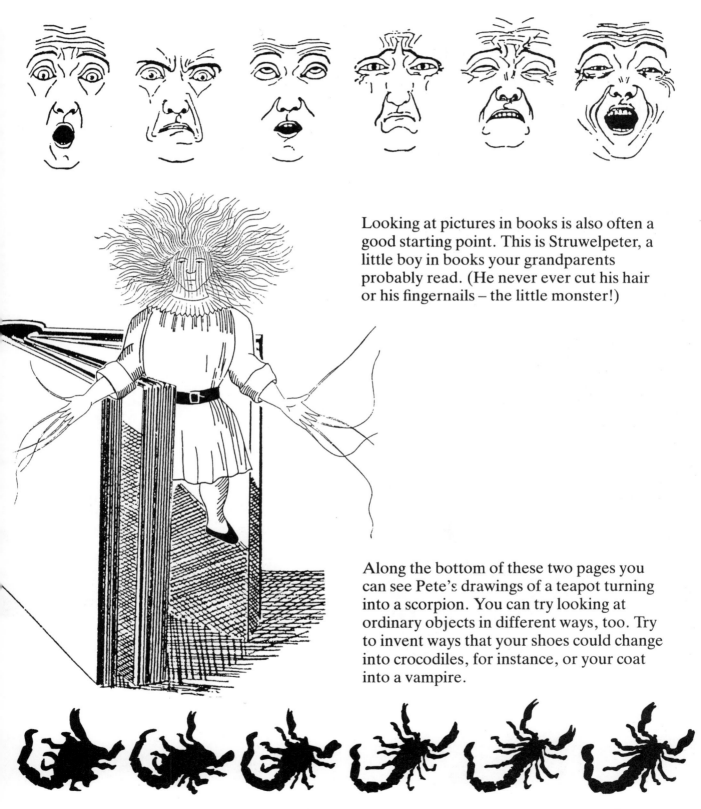

Looking at pictures in books is also often a good starting point. This is Struwelpeter, a little boy in books your grandparents probably read. (He never ever cut his hair or his fingernails – the little monster!)

Along the bottom of these two pages you can see Pete's drawings of a teapot turning into a scorpion. You can try looking at ordinary objects in different ways, too. Try to invent ways that your shoes could change into crocodiles, for instance, or your coat into a vampire.

©DIAGRAM

Part 2

What sort of paper is it best to draw on? How can you use pencils, crayons, ink or paint to get different effects? You'll find the answers to these and many other questions about drawing in this part of your book.

GETTING READY TO DRAW

As well as having the right sort of paper and tools, you need to take care over your work.

This is a pencil drawing of a fantasy creature called a griffin, about to pounce. It has an eagle's head, a lion's body and wings. Just look at those sharp claws, too! (You can find another type of griffin on pages 24–25.)

Look at the texture on the griffin's body. If you would like to know how this was done, turn to page 34 and find out how to rub it.

Pencils are excellent to draw with and there are several different types. Find out more about these on pages 24–25.

©DIAGRAM

Good places to draw

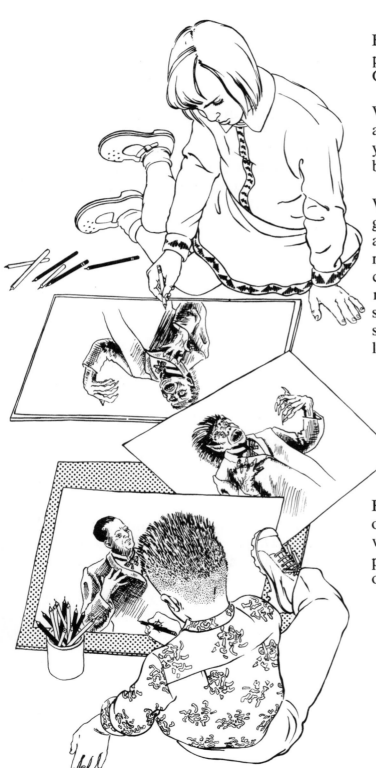

Before you get started, take a little time to prepare the space you are going to work in. Get everything ready, too.

Would you like to spend time drawing with a friend? Or would you prefer to draw on your own? Make up your mind before you begin.

Working on the floor can be fun. It will also give you lots of space so that you can lay out all the pencils, paints, pens and paper you need. (But make sure that any rug or carpet on the floor is covered with old newspaper or a plastic sheet before you start.) If you work on the floor, you can also stand up from time to time and take a good look at your drawings.

Have a hard surface like a board or a piece of cardboard on which to put the paper you will be drawing on. It is best, too, if the paper is not so large that you need to lean on it to reach a far corner.

But working on a table is sometimes a bit easier as you can get really close to your drawings when you lean forward.

Wherever you choose to work, make sure you have plenty of light. By a window may be best. If you are right-handed, try to sit so that the light from a window or a lamp comes over your left shoulder. If you are left-handed, try to arrange things so that the light comes over your right shoulder.

Reminders!

● Think about what you would like to draw before you start.

● Decide whether you will use a ballpoint, pencil, felt-tips or paints. Or perhaps you would prefer to try using ink?

● How large will your drawing be? Plan it so that it will fit the paper.

● Try not to hurry your drawing. You can always come back to it later if someone calls you away.

Which tools for different effects?

These pictures are taken from three different drawings that appear elsewhere in this book. Can you tell what they were drawn with? Find them in the book to see if you are right? (The pages to turn to are shown by each complete drawing.)

The first picture in each row, going across these two pages, is part of the whole picture at the size it was drawn. The next picture is a detail from it, shown bigger. The third picture shows the whole drawing at a small size. Each has a different effect, doesn't it?

Before you start to draw, think about the sort of effect you would like. Will you need a lot of dark areas? Would you like to be able to rub out any mistakes? Will you want to show a lot of detail? The next few pages tell you whether you should choose pencils, felt-tips, paints or a ballpoint pen once you have decided what you want your final drawing to look like.

You can either rub out your first rough pencil sketch lines, or leave them in like many artists do.

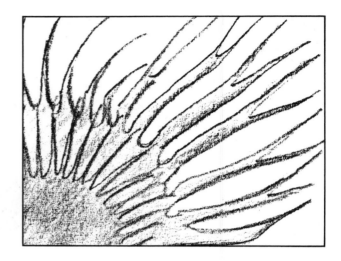

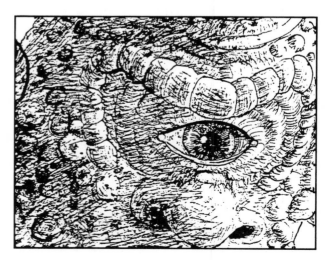

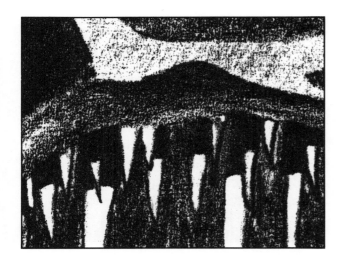

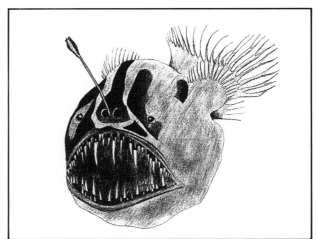

Page 132

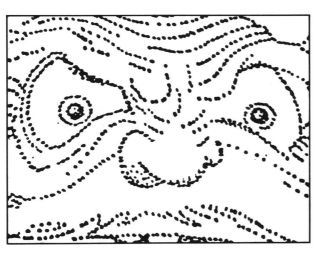

Page 97

Page 71

©DIAGRAM

Drawing with pencils

1

Most people like drawing with pencils. They are easy to use and can be rubbed out once you have planned your picture or if you make a mistake.

When you buy a pencil, you'll see it has a grade (a letter and perhaps a number, too) on the side. The scale opposite shows the whole range from a very soft 6B to a very hard 6H pencil. Soft pencils are good for dark, smudgy lines, and hard pencils are good for fine lines. Remember, too, that a soft pencil will be best for planning a drawing as it is easier to rub out.

2

Pencils work best on paper that has a rough surface. Store them in a box, or keep them in a jar with their points upward.

Always keep pencils sharpened. There should be just enough lead showing so that they will not snap when you work. Rubbing the side of your pencil lead across a sheet of sandpaper will give it a good sharp point.

These three drawings of a griffin were made with 6B, 4H and HB pencils. Can you tell which is which? You will find the answers if you turn this page upside down.

1 6B   2 4H   3 HB

3

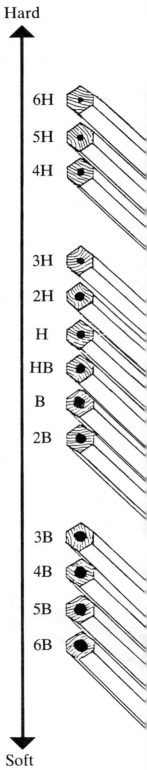

Hard

6H
5H
4H

3H
2H
H
HB
B
2B

3B
4B
5B
6B

Soft

Drawing with chalks and crayons

This mythological sphinx is made from stone and has been drawn using a sharp piece of charcoal to sketch the outline. Chalks were then used for the shaded areas. You can find another picture of a sphinx and read about its legend on page 106.

There are several different sorts of chalks and crayons. All of them smudge rather easily if you are not very careful. Use paper with a rough surface for the best results.

1 Pastel sticks come in a large number of shades and are covered in paper so that your hands don't get grubby when you pick them up.

2 Pastel pencils work a bit like lead pencils, but it is difficult to keep them sharp. This means that they are better for shading than for drawing.

3 Chalks give interesting textures, but you cannot sharpen them.

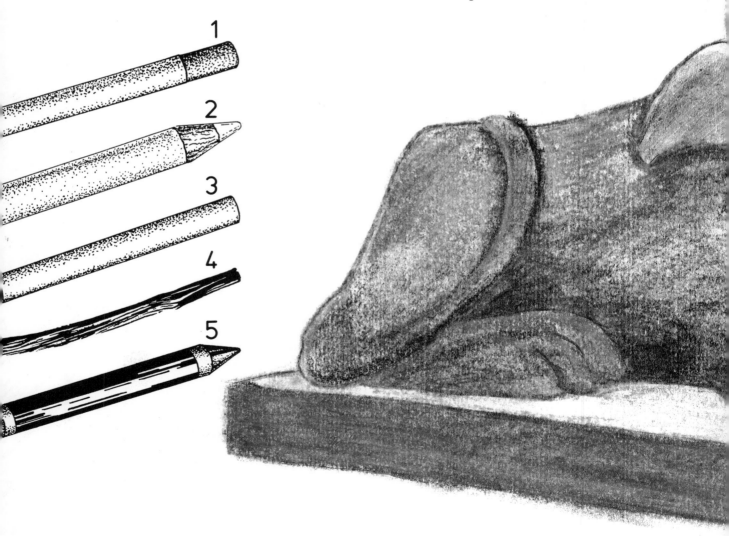

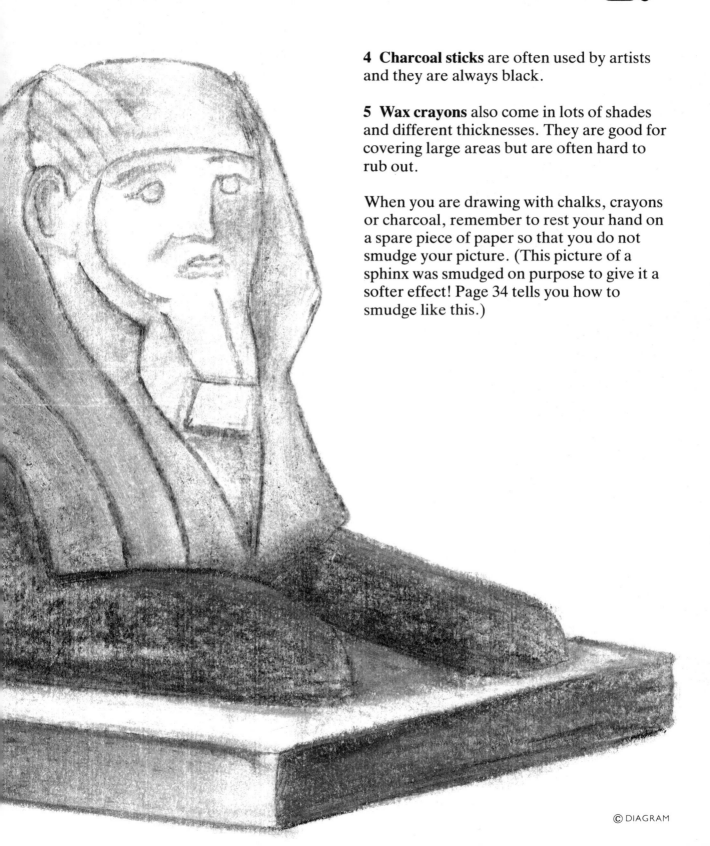

4 Charcoal sticks are often used by artists and they are always black.

5 Wax crayons also come in lots of shades and different thicknesses. They are good for covering large areas but are often hard to rub out.

When you are drawing with chalks, crayons or charcoal, remember to rest your hand on a spare piece of paper so that you do not smudge your picture. (This picture of a sphinx was smudged on purpose to give it a softer effect! Page 34 tells you how to smudge like this.)

Drawing with pens

This evil-looking snake has been drawn using four different sorts of pen – a felt-tip, a fountain pen, a ballpoint and a fat marker. The effects are very different, aren't they?

Marks made with any sort of ink do not rub out very easily. This means that if you decide to draw with ink, you need to do a pencil outline or rough sketch first before you begin your final picture. You can, of course, also trace using ink.

Ink will not give you the chance to shade like you can when you use a pencil or crayons. So if you use a pen to do your drawing, you will have to build up darker areas in your picture with lots of dots or criss-cross lines.

Remember to replace the tops on your felt-tips when you are not using them or the ink may dry up.

Try to keep ink off your hands while you are drawing or you may get blotches and fingermarks all over your pictures.
Take care, as well, not to spill any ink if you are using a fountain pen or dip pen. And try not to get it on your clothes.

Using brushes

This terrifying werewolf was drawn with a paintbrush and black ink. Brushes come in different thicknesses. As you can see below, larger ones will give a very different effect from small ones. Use a thick brush for painting large areas in a big picture. It will help you finish your drawing more quickly. Use a thinner brush for fine detail. The very best brushes are made from sable or squirrel hair; but cheaper ones can be very good, too.

Use your brushes gently. Don't put too much paint on them either, or you may get blotches everywhere.

Wash all your brushes after you have used them, and store them in a jar so that the brush ends point upward. This will prevent them from becoming damaged.

Use strong paper when you work with a brush. If you paint on very thin paper, your drawing may curl up.

Notice how the werewolf's hairs grow in different directions on different parts of its face. The huge teeth and pointed, staring eyes help to make him look particularly frightening.

A werewolf's head would make a good subject for a mask. Turn to page 64 to find out how to make one.

©DIAGRAM

Choosing paper

The sort of paper you should use depends on whether you are working with a pencil, inks or paint. If you use very thin paper, for instance, you cannot work with paints as the paper may curl up.

If you use thick paper, you cannot trace a drawing. But you could transfer a tracing onto the thick paper, using the method on pages 42–43.

Tracing paper
It is always useful to have some thin paper that you can see through. This will be helpful because you can learn a lot by tracing pictures of monsters from books. You can also trace drawings you have already made.

Looking after your paper
A lot of people throw away good paper that you might use for drawing. If someone in your family does this, see if you can rescue it. Even small pieces are useful for rough sketches. Save them until the next time you draw.

Keep all your drawing paper flat. If it comes in a roll, simply curl it back the other way to stop it from curling up again.

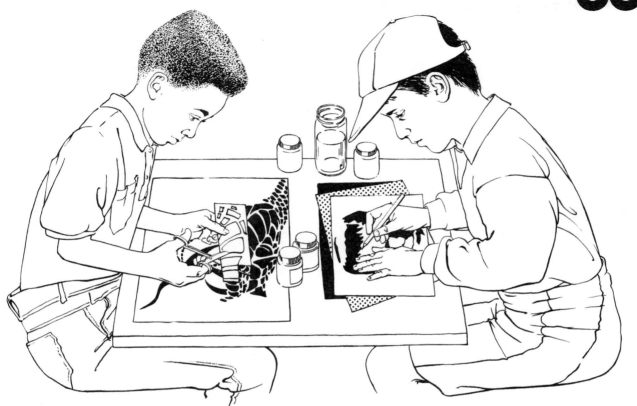

Points to remember about paper
- Tracing paper is very useful if you want to copy drawings from books. You can also use it to transfer drawings onto cardboard or thick paper. But you cannot use a paintbrush on tracing paper very well.
- Smooth paper is usually good for felt-tips. But it is not very strong, so it is best not to use water-paints on this sort of paper.
- Some papers, which you can buy in an art shop, come in lots of different shades other than white, and will usually take paint.
- Strong drawing paper is also sold in art shops and will usually have a rough surface. This means it is good for pencils, inks and paints.
- The thickness of a paper is called its "weight". So when you buy paper, you can ask for a heavyweight or lightweight sort.

Drawing pads
You can buy paper in single sheets at an art shop. But you can also buy drawing pads. These are often a good idea as it means you can keep all your pictures together in one place.

Making textures

Giving the effect of texture to your drawings, so that you can almost feel what it would be like to stroke a monster (if you dared), is easier than it seems. There are lots of ways to do it.

Find a piece of sandpaper and run your hand over it. Rough, isn't it? Now try to find a piece of silk and rub your hand over that. You can feel the difference, can't you?

What you are feeling is known as texture. The sandpaper and the silk look very different and they also have a different texture if you run your fingers over them.

Enjoy experimenting with texture! But I suggest you try out everything on a piece of scrap paper first before you give texture to your final drawing.

Smudge it!
If you work on strong paper with pencils or chalks, you can rub or smudge parts of your drawing with a finger or a tissue – not by accident but on purpose – to get a softer effect, just as we did with the drawing of the sphinx on pages 26–27.

Rub it!
If you draw on thin paper, after you have finished your outline, place it over a rough surface (a plank of wood or some fabric perhaps) and then rub crayon across the area you want to cover. This will give you a texture just like the wood or fabric that you put underneath the paper. (Turn back to the griffin on pages 18–19 to see this effect.)

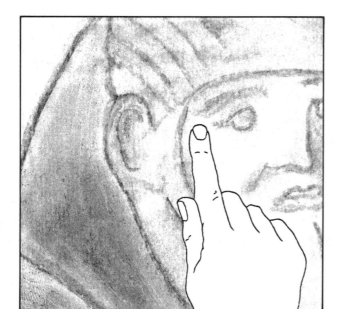

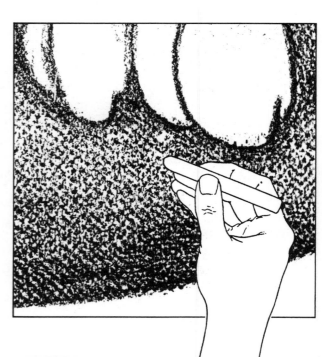

Scrape it!
You can sometimes scrape off parts of a drawing if you have worked with paint or ink on very strong paper. This will give the effect of a creature with very rough skin. You can use a nail file for this. You will find examples on pages 37 and 73.

Splatter it!
This is fun. When you have finished the outline of any monster you are drawing, cut it out and put it on some old newspaper. Find an old toothbrush that you are sure no one wants anymore. Dip the brush into ink or paint, and splatter a spray at the drawing, flicking off the paint with a small stick. (It is best to wear a smock when you do this.)

Dab it!
If you work with a pen and ink, you can carefully dab the edges of your drawing with a wet tissue to give a softer effect. But be sure to work with strong paper if you try this out; a wet tissue may make a hole in thin paper.

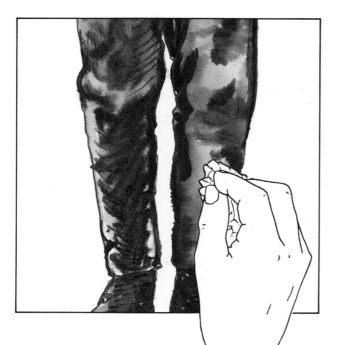

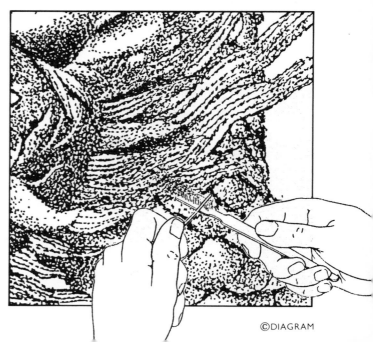

Creating special effects – 1

Scratch it!

If you would like to make a picture of a really spooky ghost, first take a sheet of smooth white paper and colour it using a thick, black wax crayon. You might need to go over the paper twice to get a good finish.

Next, sketch your picture of a ghost or demon on a different piece of white paper. Using masking tape to fix your drawing over your black waxy paper, and use a sharp pencil to go over your picture. When you remove the white paper, you should find an outline on the waxy surface underneath.

Now use a nail file or a knitting needle to scratch away at the picture. (Take care as you do this – pointed objects can be very dangerous.)

Turn to pages 40–41, 72–73 and 128 for more examples of white on black pictures.

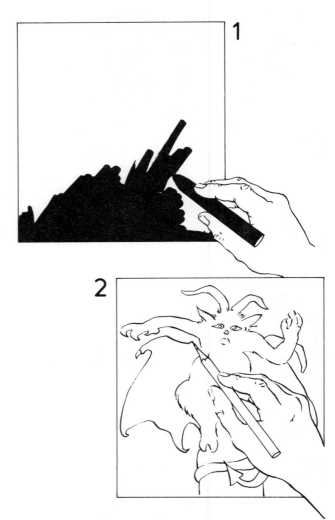

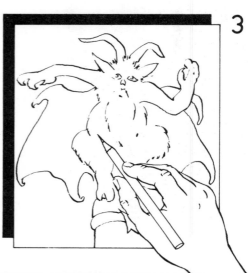

Special effects – 2

Lighting

Take a look at the large skull below or the one on page 56. Now try to imagine a bright light shining on the skull from above, from one side or from the front

Can you tell which direction the light was coming from in each of the six other drawings of skulls on these two pages?

Your drawings of monsters will always look more dramatic if you shade in those areas that are in shadow.

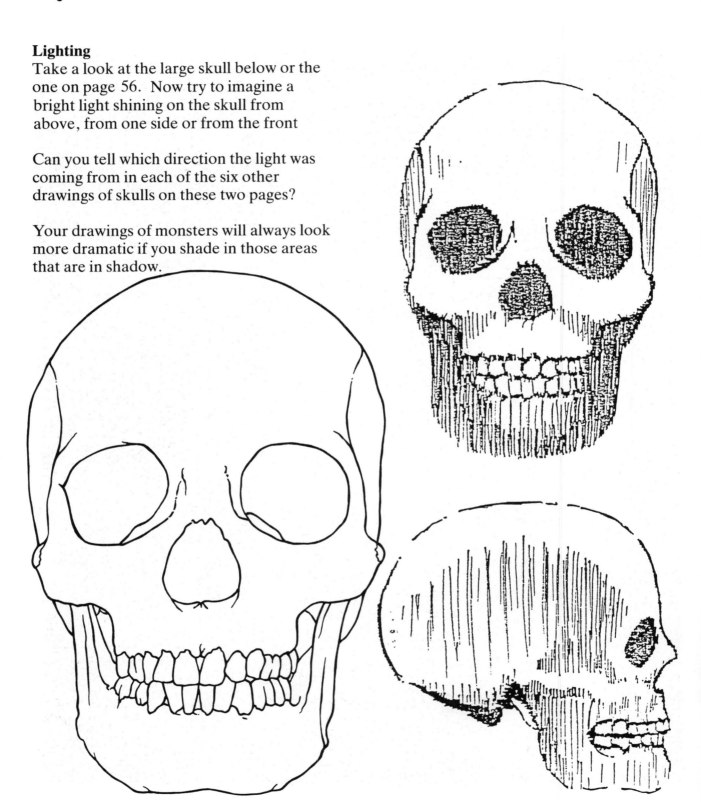

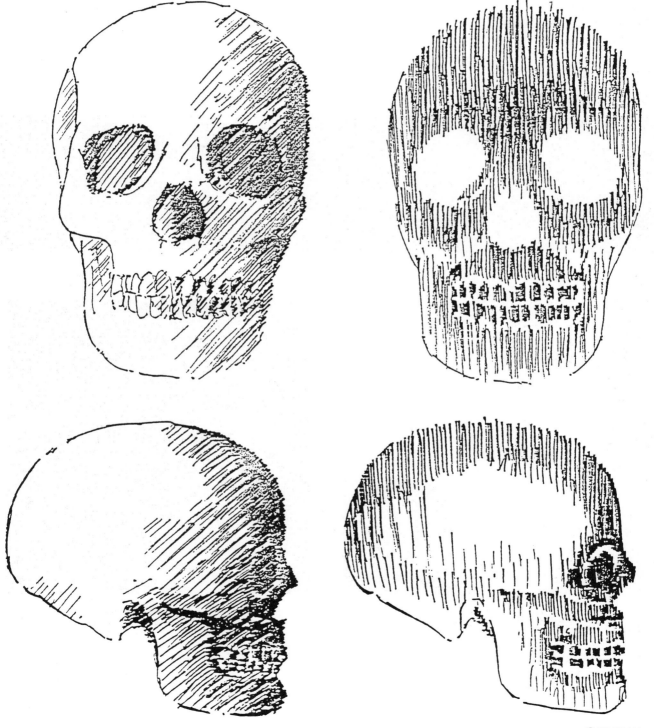

White on black

It can be great fun to draw or paint in white on black paper, and the effects can be very exciting. Just look at that giant spider opposite! Some people scream whenever they see one.
Look back at its cousin on page 10, too.

You can copy it, and then draw a web for the background by following the five steps shown. Use blobs of white paint if you would like to make the web look as if it is covered in early morning dew.

A spider's web usually has a neat pattern. Begin with a square and then divide this up into parts from the middle, so that you have a sketch that looks like a bicycle wheel. Then weave a line between the spokes.

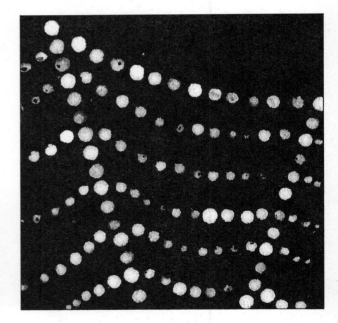

Tracing

Sometimes it can help to trace an outline of a monster from a book. You can then add your own shading and details. A pencil will usually be best for tracing, but you can also use a ballpoint or a felt-tip.

You can trace any of the pictures in this book. To help you start, here is a drawing of a monster whose legs, head and body come from lots of different creatures.

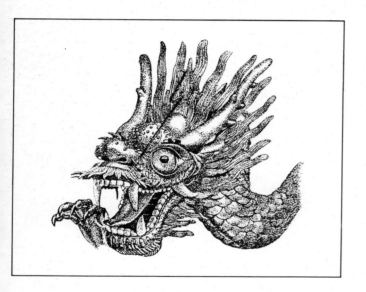

If you would like to transfer a tracing onto another piece of paper or cardboard, you can do this easily using the following method.

First cover the picture with clear tracing paper and fix this to the page with the sort of tape that peels off without leaving a mark. This is usually called masking tape.

Do not use ordinary sticky tape – it will damage the book.

Using a sharp pencil, now draw round the main shape. You can also trace any of the details you think it may be hard to copy later.

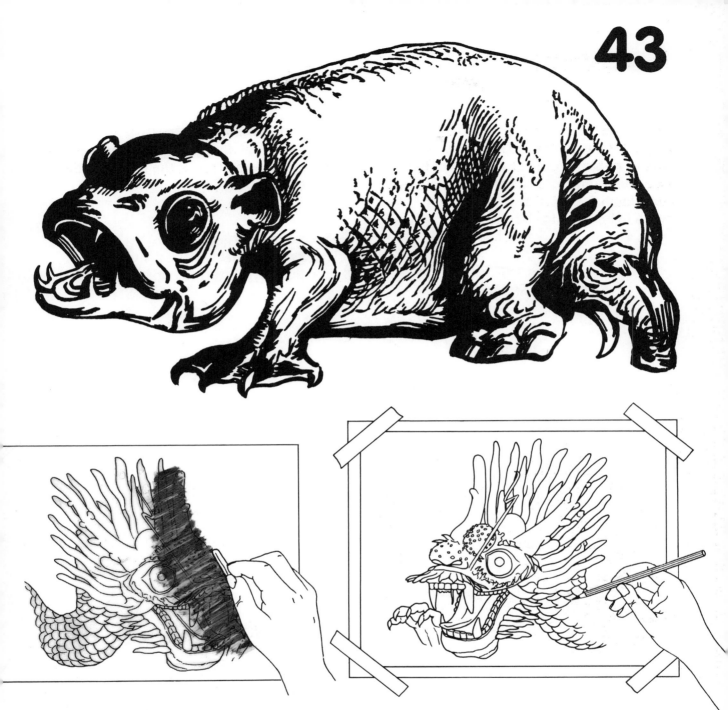

Now remove the tracing paper. Turn it over, and rub with a soft pencil (grade B) on to the lines that show through to the back of the tracing paper. Turn the tracing paper back again to its right side. Now put it on a piece of paper or cardboard. This time, use a hard pencil (grade 2H) with a sharp point and go over all the lines quite firmly but not too hard.

When you take the tracing paper away, you should find you have a shadow of the drawing on the paper or cardboard beneath it. You can use these ghost lines to help with your own drawing.

Remember not to press too hard when you trace as you may spoil the picture you are copying.

© DIAGRAM

Copying

Copying drawings will give you lots of ideas for your own pictures. Try hard to get the shapes right or your copies will not look like the originals. Of course, if you use a pencil and the original was done in ink, the two will be very different.

Here are some useful tips to help you master the art of copying. Try them out as you copy the picture of the three-headed dragon opposite.

Plan your drawing
Using a soft pencil, draw the basic shape first before you start to copy any detail.

1

Then build on your basic shapes, adding the head, wing, tail and feet details.

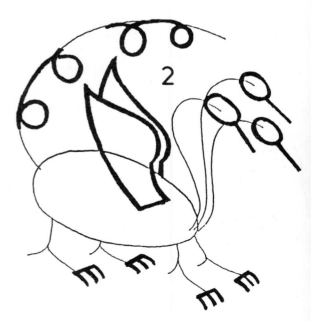

2

As you work on your copy, keep checking that the spaces between the various parts of the dragon's body are in proportion to the original.

3

Keep checking your drawing
When you are copying, keep looking back
at the original drawing to check you are
putting everything in the right place.
Check, too, that you have the right number
of claws on each foot and four loops in the
tail. Don't forget the arrow shapes at the
ends of the three tongues, and notice how
the body scales overlap.

Scale

There is also a way you can make your drawings of monsters look very much bigger. This gigantic praying mantis is really just an insect, like the one in the boy's hand opposite: but he seems to be huge because, by the side of him, we have drawn a tiny man. It is all a matter of what artists call scale. We expect the man to be much bigger than the insect. If, instead, we make the insect very much bigger than the man, it becomes a monster.

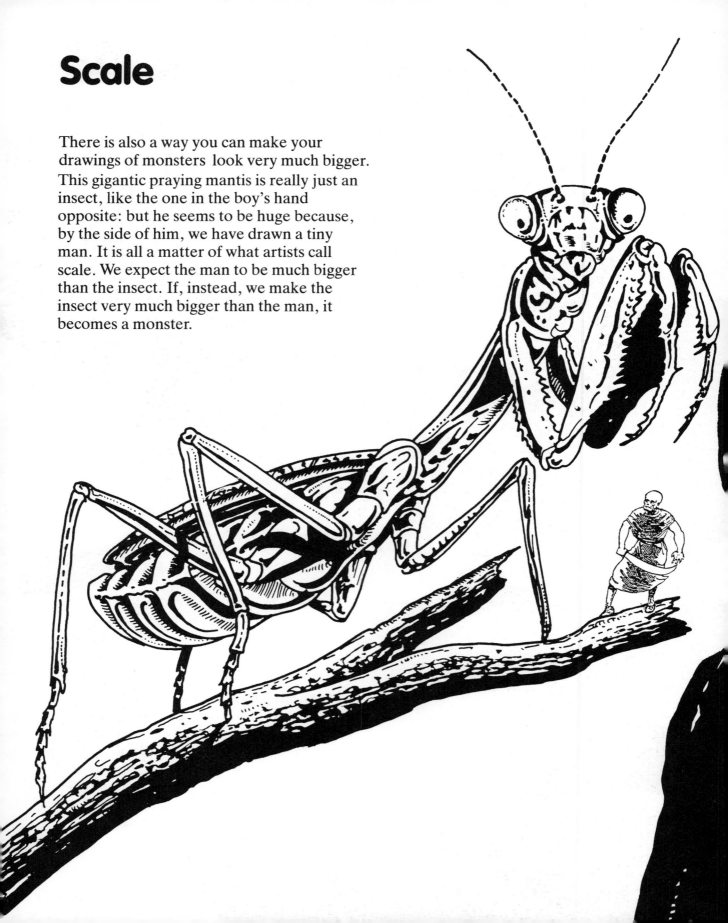

Comic book artists very often use this trick.
Here is a boy surprised to see a tiny man on
the branch of a tree.

Changing the size

It is easy to change the size of your drawing or any picture you are copying from a book by using squares.

First turn the drawing you would like to enlarge upside down so that the top of the picture is now at the bottom. This will help you to concentrate when you copy the outline. Then trace the drawing using a pencil.

Next draw squares over your tracing, as shown, using a ruler for straight lines. Draw them down your tracing paper and then across. Make sure all lines are the same distance apart.

Now take a large sheet of paper and again draw squares. But this time make the squares larger than those on the tracing paper. (If you want to reduce the size of the picture, use a smaller piece of paper and draw smaller squares than on your tracing paper.) Be sure to draw the same number of squares. This is important whether you want to make your drawing bigger or smaller. If there are 24 squares on your tracing paper, there must be 24 squares on the other piece of paper.

Next, copy the tracing onto the other piece of paper, matching carefully what is in each square. For example, the third square from the left at the top of the tracing paper should exactly match the third square from the left at the top of your drawing paper.

Watch where the lines of the picture cross each square on the tracing paper. Make them cross at exactly the same points on the larger (or smaller) squares of your drawing paper.

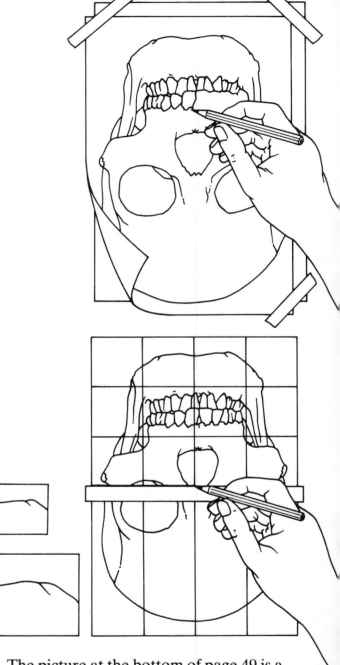

The picture at the bottom of page 49 is a copy of the drawing on pages 90–91, at a smaller size. Do you know who it is meant to be?

On page 140, there are some squares that you can trace with a pencil and ruler to enlarge this drawing or others in the book.

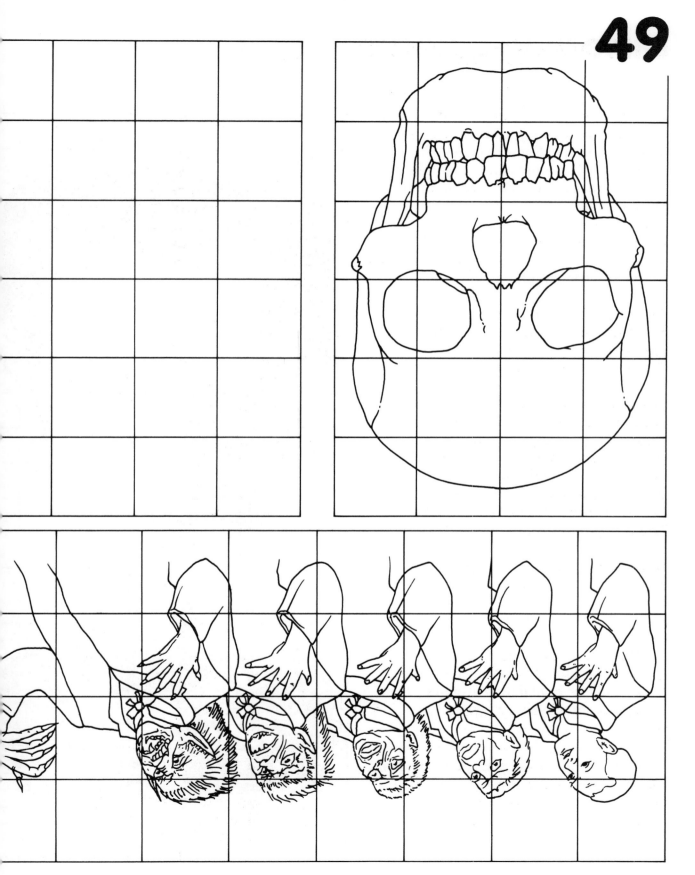

Distorting a head

Have you ever seen yourself in the sort of distorting mirror they have at fairgrounds and other places? Some make you look enormously fat; others make you long and lean. You can do the same sort of thing with your drawings.

There are three different ways in which you can distort your pictures to make them look even more frightening.

You can, for instance, draw a picture of Frankenstein's monster, as described on pages 62–63, and then add squares by drawing lines from top to bottom and across your piece of paper, using a ruler. With a pencil, you can now draw rectangles on another piece of paper. These should be shapes that are longer and thinner than squares. Then copy the drawing of Frankenstein's monster, using the method described on pages 48–49. Next rub out the rectangles. The face will now be much longer and more pointed.

In the same way, you can copy your original picture of Frankenstein's monster onto rectangles that are wider than squares, and get a much broader face.

Another method of distortion involves cutting your finished drawing into strips, moving these about and then gluing them down on another sheet of paper.

The spooky mummy opposite is the drawing on page 61, which has been cut up. The bits have then been stuck down in a crooked way to give the effect of distortion.

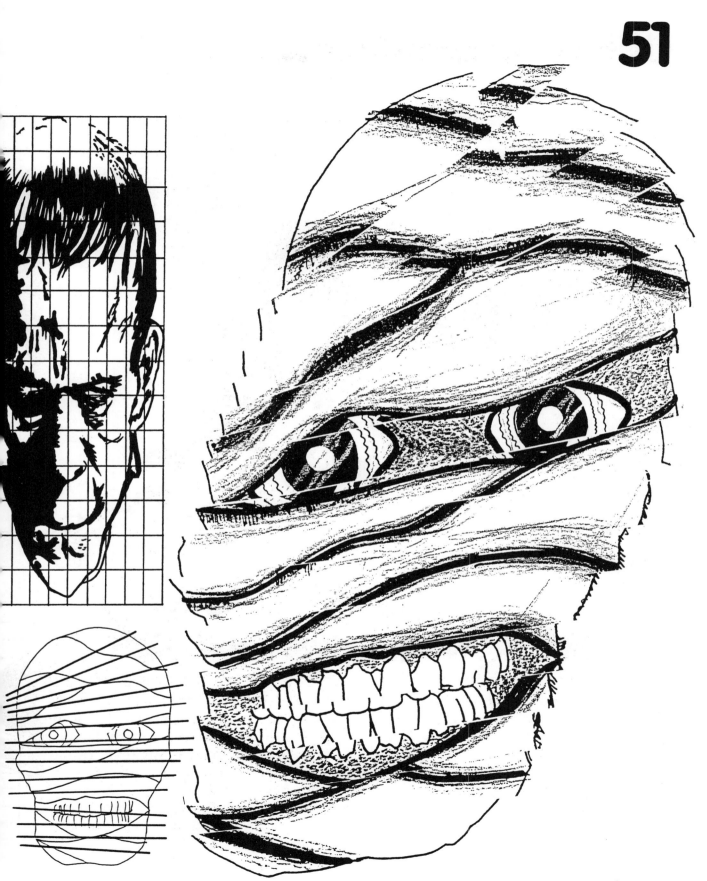

Using your drawings

There are lots of amusing things you can do with your drawings of monsters when you have finished them. So think about how you would like to use your pictures before you start to draw them. Here are some ideas. You can make a frieze by drawing rows of all different kinds of monsters along a roll of paper. Or you could draw some monsters on cardboard, cut them out and use the shapes left as stencils. Using masking tape, fix them to a roll of paper and fill in the cut-out areas with a felt-tip or paint, as shown. You could then put up the frieze on the wall of your room.

Try cutting out simple monster shapes and making them into mobiles to hang up with a thread or some wire from the ceiling. It will be best to draw on cardboard rather than paper for this, and to get an adult to help you put up the mobile.

You can also make very detailed drawings of monsters to display on the wall as posters or to fix to the door of your room. Don't forget to sign your drawings when you have finished them, either with your initials or your whole name in one corner. Perhaps put the date, too. If your drawings are really good, you could ask if you can have them framed.

Monster cards are fun to make for birthdays. If you are sending out party invitations, these could have a monster theme, too. There could be a drawing with a message underneath or you can make a folded card with a picture on the front and a written message inside. Make sure you have the right size envelopes before you start.

You could even make your own comic strips about a monster adventure which your friends might enjoy reading. Visit the library and bookshops and find out all you can about monsters in science fiction.

You can also play a monster game with two or more friends. Each player has a sheet of paper and draws a monster's head at the top of the sheet. Keep your drawings secret! Then each of you should fold over the top of the paper and pass it on to the person on the right, who should add a monster body without looking at the head. Fold the papers again, and pass them on again to the right. Each of you should now draw in some monster legs. The results should be very funny indeed!

Part 3

DRAWING MONSTERS' HEADS

Over the next few pages, I am going to show
you how easy it is to produce sensational
drawings of the heads of monsters that are as
terrifying as the dragon opposite and the shark below.

Horrific heads

You can find out how to draw all the
monster heads shown here over the next
few pages. Which one do you think is the
most horrific? My knees would probably go
really wobbly if I met the vampire or the
cyclops on a dark night. Do you know
which they are?

©DIAGRAM

A human skull

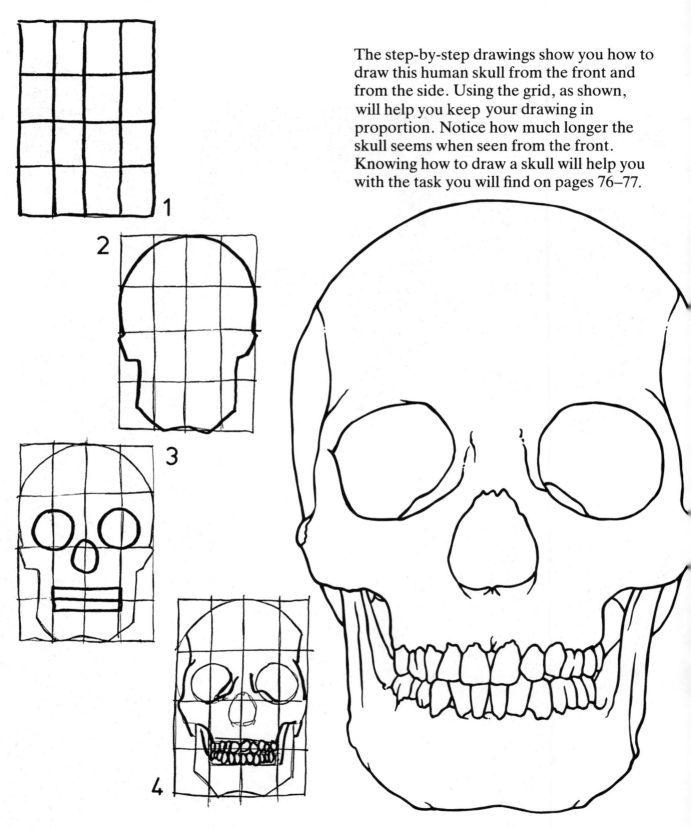

The step-by-step drawings show you how to draw this human skull from the front and from the side. Using the grid, as shown, will help you keep your drawing in proportion. Notice how much longer the skull seems when seen from the front. Knowing how to draw a skull will help you with the task you will find on pages 76–77.

1

2

3

4

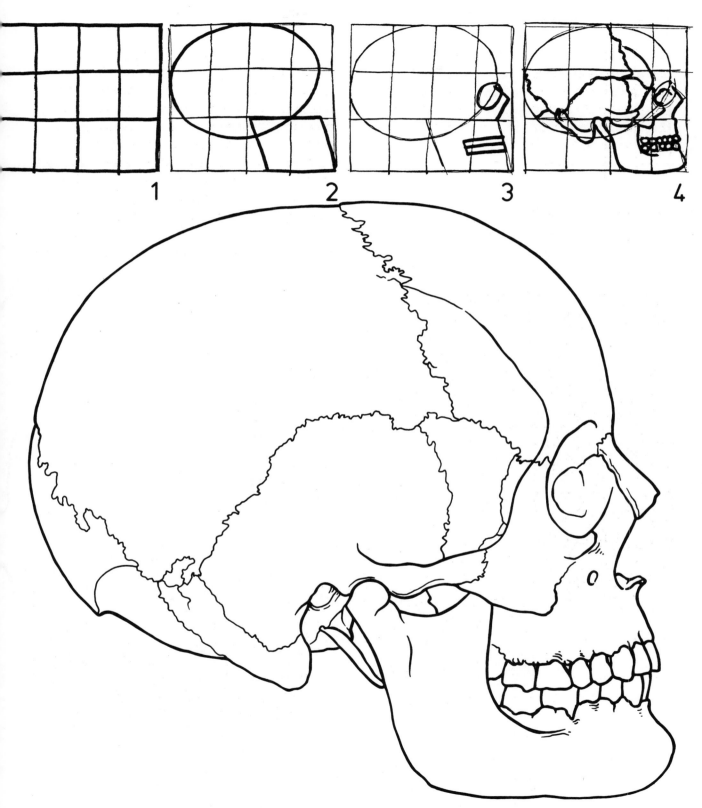

1

2

3

4

©DIAGRAM

A mummy's face

Do you know what a mummy is, when it is not a female parent? In ancient Egypt, they used to preserve the bodies of the dead and wrap them up in bandages. The bodies were then known as mummies, whether they were male or female.

You can draw the face of a mummy by following the three stages shown here. Don't forget to leave the teeth white, and make the eyes seem to stare so that your picture will be more scary. You can give texture to the skin by rubbing a pink, yellow, brown or black crayon over a rough surface like the cover of a hardcover book or a stone. The textures shown below were made by rubbing a crayon onto paper placed over a book, a stone, and a piece of wood. Can you tell which is which?

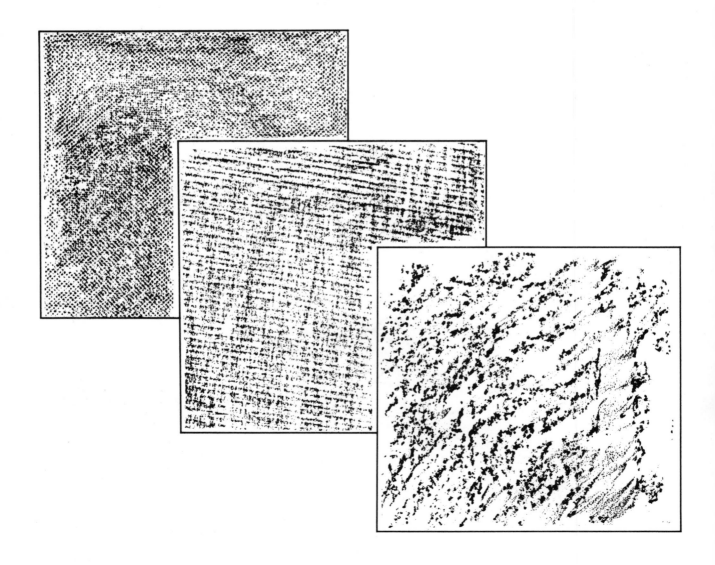

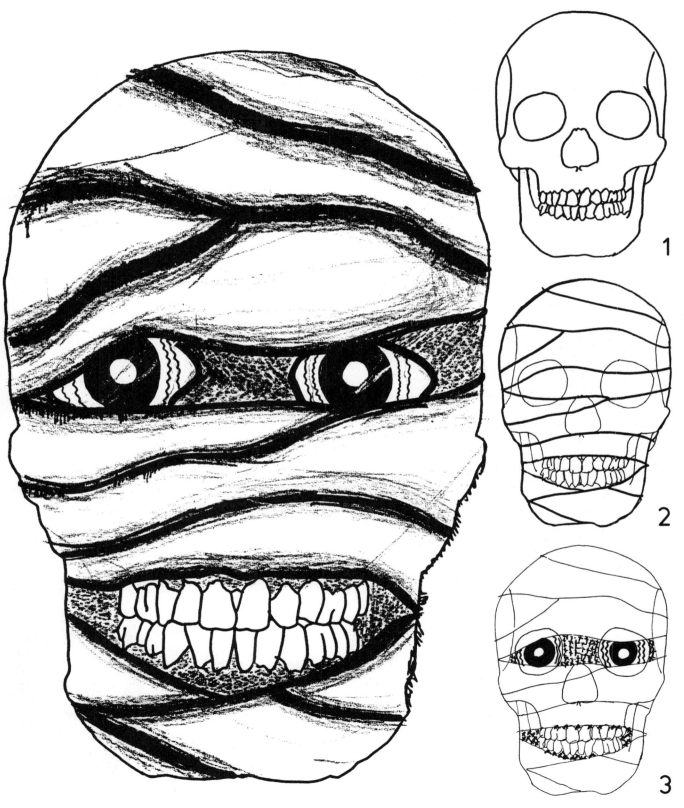

1

2

3

Frankenstein's monster

Follow the step-by-step stages to produce this head of Frankenstein's artificial man, which you can read about in Mary Shelley's book or which you might see one day in a film when you are older. This awful creature terrorized everyone and even killed a number of people. He looks really evil, doesn't he? But, of course, he only existed in Mary Shelley's imagination. Why not try to create some monsters of your own?

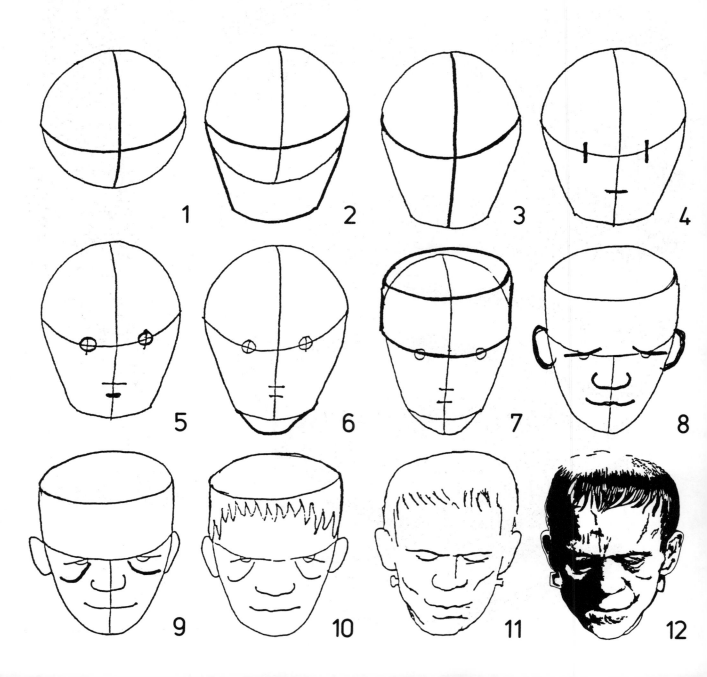

This is a felt-tip pen drawing.

A very wicked witch

You might like to make a witch mask to wear on Hallowe'en. Simply draw the witch's head about the same size as your face, using thin cardboard rather than paper. Then cut it out carefully and make two small holes, one on each side just above where your ears will be, by pushing through with a knitting needle. (Remember to take care with sharp objects.) Thread through two pieces of string, one on each side. They should be long enough to tie into a knot at the back of your head. Of course, you can also make masks using any of the other faces in this book.

This wicked-looking witch is really very ugly, isn't she? Just look how two of her front teeth stick out, her great big nose and her very lined face! The holes in her cheeks are for string to go through when you tie the mask round your face.

You could also make a werewolf mask from the face on page 31.

A vampire

Count Dracula lived in a lonely castle in Transylvania, part of Romania. He was the main character in Bram Stoker's book and is possibly the most famous vampire of all. They say that vampires hate garlic, so if you hang some up at home, it may be a bit smelly, but you should not be troubled by these bloodthirsty creatures. (But they don't really exist – or do they?

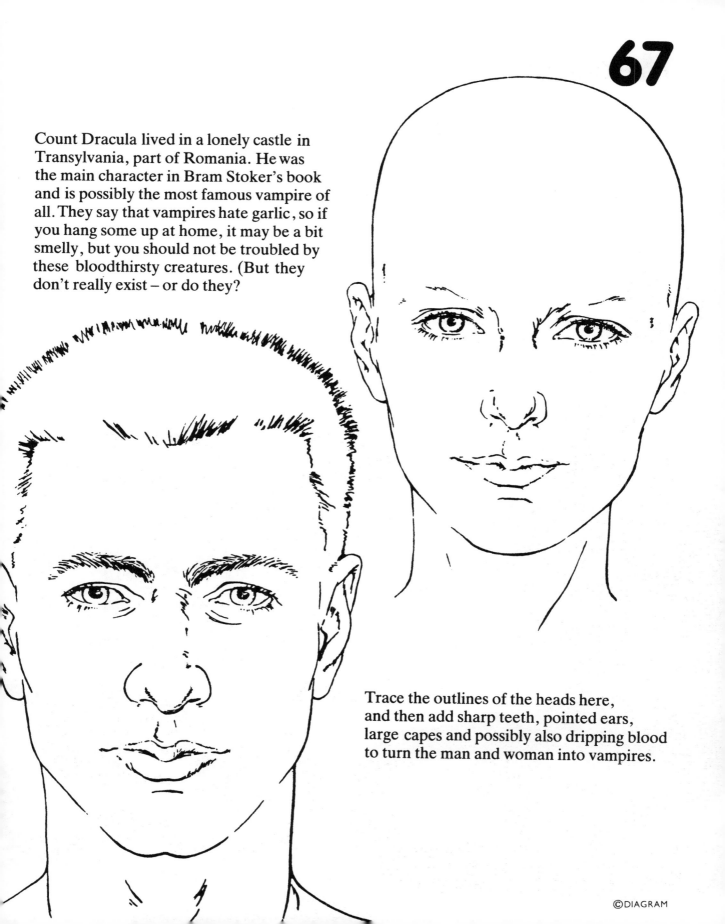

Trace the outlines of the heads here, and then add sharp teeth, pointed ears, large capes and possibly also dripping blood to turn the man and woman into vampires.

©DIAGRAM

Medusa

How would you like to have all these snakes in place of your hair? I think it would be terribly uncomfortable, don't you? Medusa, a woman in an ancient Greek legend who was supposed to be able to turn you into stone if you looked into her eyes, had a whole head of snakes.

To draw her, first copy a picture of a woman's face. You should be able to find one to copy from in a magazine. Or you could adapt one of the faces on the page before this. Then add snakes for the hair.

Some of the snakes could be plain, others could be patterned with markings. Here are some for you to copy. Be sure to make Medusa's eyes stare.

The cyclops

The cyclops was a one-eyed, one-horned horrific giant who appears in the legends of Greek mythology.

The step-by-step drawings below show how easily you can build up this fierce and very ugly face from a simple circle.

The cyclops opposite was drawn with a ballpoint pen but you could use crayons, felt-tips or a pencil, if you like. Plan your drawing with a soft pencil first. To make the skin look rough, make lots of marks, scribbles and blobs. Don't forget to make the teeth very pointed and add long nails.

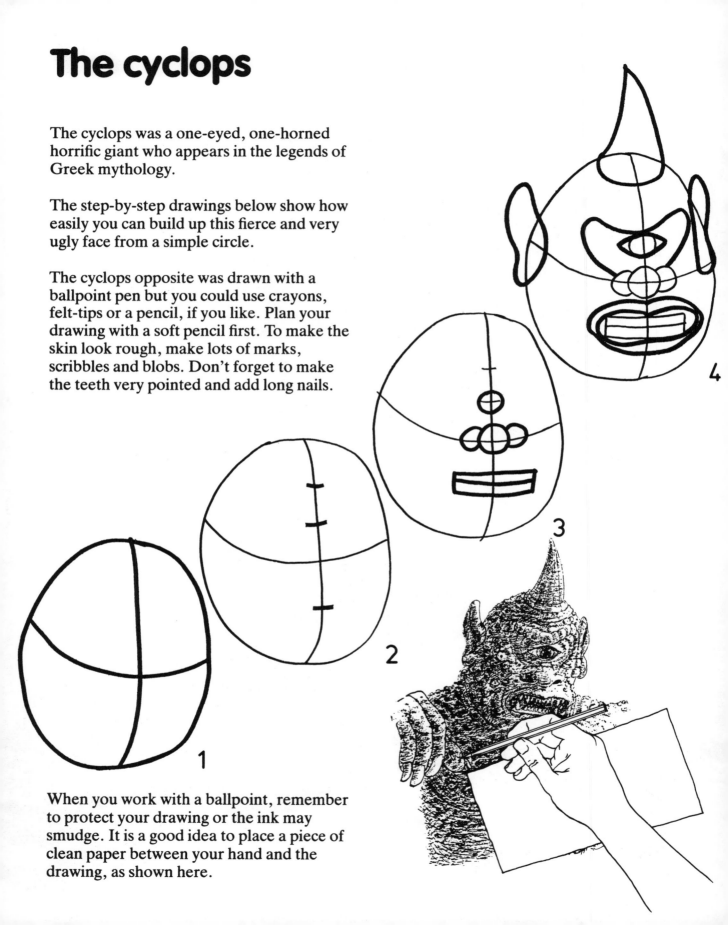

When you work with a ballpoint, remember to protect your drawing or the ink may smudge. It is a good idea to place a piece of clean paper between your hand and the drawing, as shown here.

71

5

©DIAGRAM

An evil demon

This supernatural spirit has pointed ears, slanting eyes, big horns and a deeply dimpled chin. Follow the step-by-step stages, and you will soon find you have a drawing so terrifying that it might make your hair stand on end!

Ryozo shaded in this demon with a black wax crayon, and then scratched away at the surface with a needle to give texture to the face. This made the paper very smudgy. So he cut out his drawing and stuck it onto another sheet. This gave his picture a sharp, fresh outline.

This could make a good mask.

A dragon's head

The mythological monster opposite is like a snake with a most unusual head, and is said to breathe fire. It is often found in Eastern paintings, particularly in China, and many stories tell how the dragon lived in the water but in spring used its wings to fly up to the clouds.

Lee used pictures of lizards and snakes to help him draw the dragon's skin and a picture of a tiger to help with the dragon's four pointed teeth.

You can either follow the step-by-step stages below, or trace the outline opposite and then add the details.

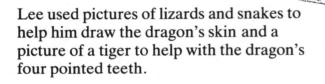

1   2   3   4

5   6   7

Make your own scary head

Putting one picture over another is called superimposing. On the right for example, there is an old picture of a skull with a portrait of a pair of twins that has been superimposed on it.

Below, you can see how Jeremy has drawn a portrait of himself by looking in the mirror, and then superimposing a snarling tiger, a monkey and a bird on his head. He copied these from a wildlife magazine.

On the right-hand page, you can also see how he made a very ghoulish self-portrait by tracing a skull and adding a self-portrait to it. To make a scary head that looks like you, first draw a skull, and then add your facial details while looking in a mirror. Be sure to let some of the lines of the skull show through, particularly the teeth and eye sockets.

Part 4

Monsters from the grave, monsters from under the microscope, monsters from mythology, and monsters from the movies: here are thirty – one ghoulish creatures. Are you brave enough to flick through these pages and then pick up a pencil and create your own?

The first twelve monsters all have human forms, but how strange they are! Unlike you or I, they lived in the imagination of writers and artists.

You will find many monsters with animal bodies on the pages that follow, too, as well as one made entirely of mud!

Have fun copying them, but also add some ideas of your own.

On the left, there are seven monster figures which you will find elsewhere in this book, and opposite there are five bodies risen from their graves. Bring them to life with a pencil and paper!

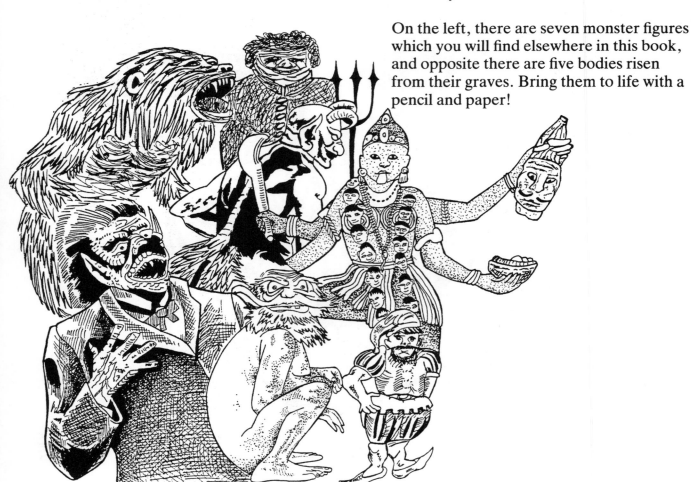

YOUR MONSTER HORROR SHOW

A scary skeleton

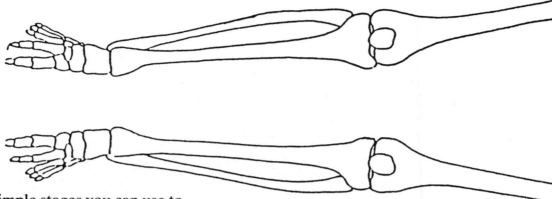

Here are eight simple stages you can use to produce a really scary skeleton. Start with a stick person. Then mark the joints. Add the rib cage and pelvis, and next put in the bones. Notice how thin the bones are, but that they widen at the joints. Try to keep the body in proportion. The arms, for instance, should be about the same length as the legs; and, of course, the thumbs are shorter than the other fingers. Remember, too, that the ribs are above where the stomach would be. Perhaps then give the skeleton a name. How about Harold, or Ermintrude for a girl? Turn the book on its side to look at the picture above.

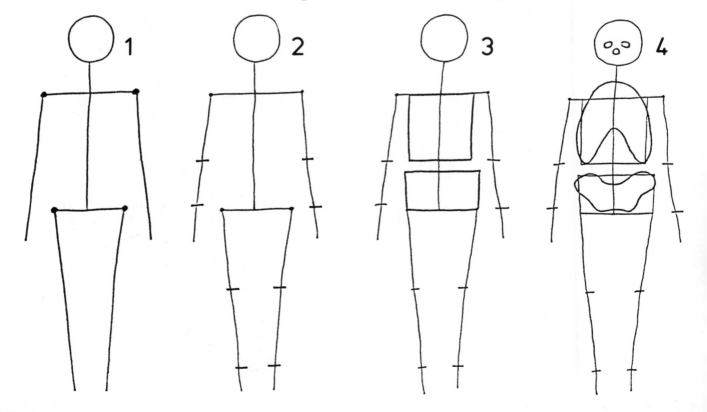

5

6

7

8

Zombies

Zombies are strange figures that sometimes rise up from the dead and then walk about mindlessly, as if in a dream.

Here is a whole family of zombie monsters below, drawn in ink. Notice how the eyes have been left white to make them look more frightening.

You can make the misty swamp at the bottom of the picture by painting white streaks across the page.

The outline of the first figure here was traced by Paul from a mail order magazine. Then he drew three more similar figures, but each time made the clothes more ragged, the hair longer and the hands bonier.

You can make eerie blobs by blowing (through a drinking straw) at the ink or paint on your drawing while it is still wet.

An Egyptian mummy

On pages 60–61, you saw how to draw a mummy's face. Now it's time to draw the whole body, which is like the figure below but completely wrapped in bandages.

First draw a stick figure as shown. Then gradually give it shaped arms and legs. Finally, add the strips of bandage that go all the way round the body, including the fingers and toes, so that no part is exposed.

This is what a mummy would look like without bandages.

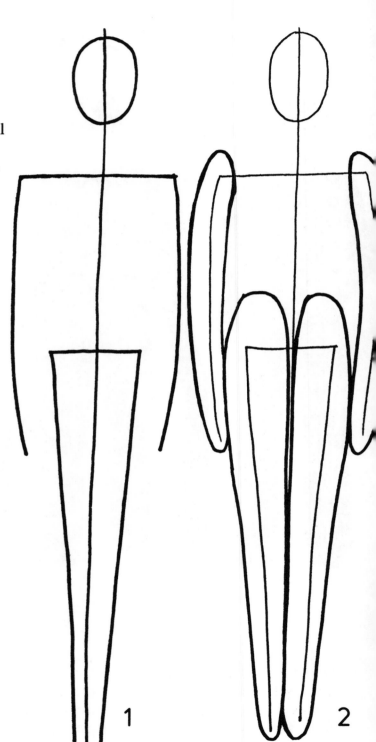

1

2

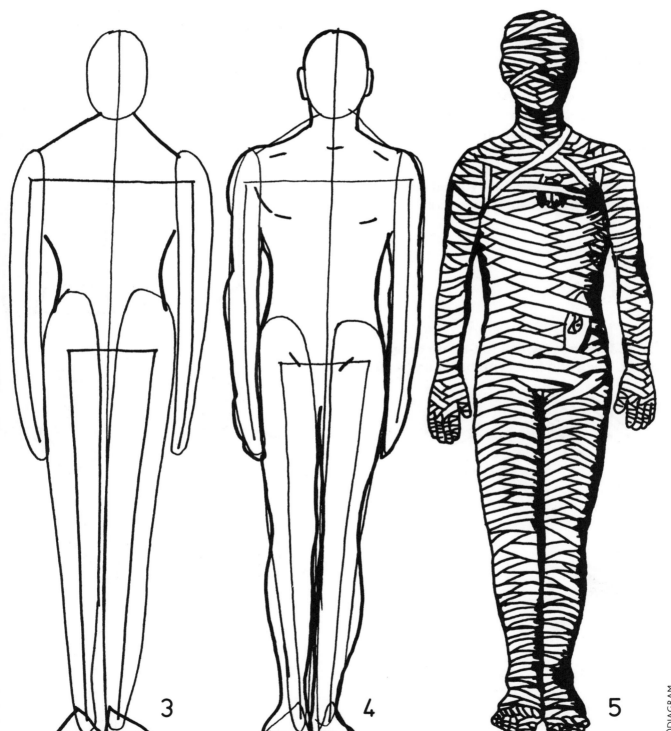

3

4

5

Frankenstein's monster – full length

The weird artificial man opposite was drawn in felt-tip. Water was then added to make the suit seem thicker. Look how large the hands, feet and shoulders are, and how flat the top of the monster's head is.

First draw a simple outline of a man and square off and enlarge the head, shoulders, arms and feet. You can then add all the other details.

Look back to pages 62–63 to find another portrait of Frankenstein's creation.

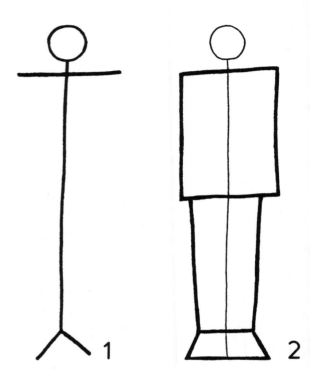

Draw dark areas with a felt-tip on rough paper. Then add tone with brush and water.

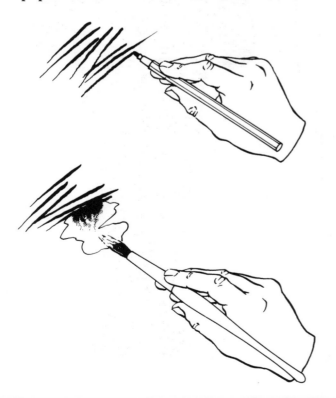

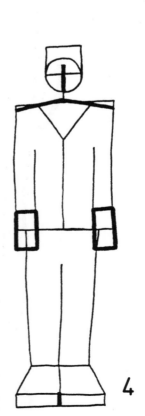

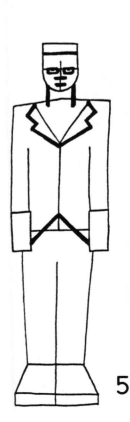

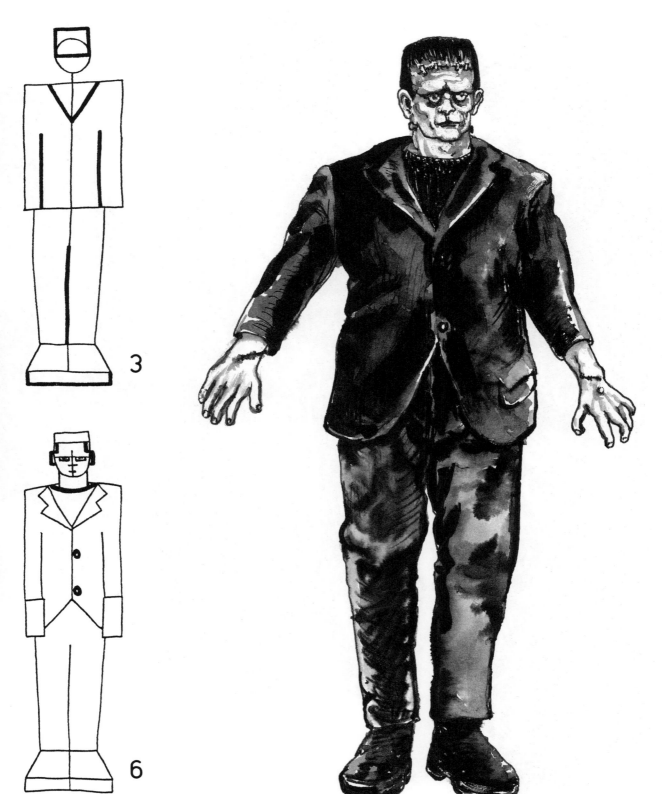

3

6

A vampire turns into a bat

In these five drawings, Pauline has shown a vampire turning through various stages into a bat. How spooky! Notice how the head and body shrink in each drawing, and the cloak gradually turns into the bat's wings.

You can find out about Count Dracula and how to draw other vampires on pages 66–67.

Pauline began by sketching the basic shapes with a soft pencil. Then she filled in the dark areas with a dark wax crayon. Using the pointed end of a knitting needle, she then scratched out white lines. Finally, she added detail to the faces with a felt-tip pen. Her original drawings have been enlarged on the left so that you can see their texture clearly.

©DIAGRAM

Dr Jekyll and Mr Hyde

In his famous science fiction story, Robert Louis Stevenson makes the charming Dr Jekyll turn into the monstrous Mr Hyde.

The pictures here show the transformation in five stages and were drawn using a fountain pen.

Before you start, take your pen and try to make as many different types of mark as you can. The drawings above include lots of cross-hatching on Dr Jekyll's/Mr Hyde's jacket: these are lines which cross each other to create texture.

Who would you prefer lived next door to you – Dr Jekyll or Mr Hyde?

Opposite are three heads. Try to redraw them, turning each into a monster in five different stages.

A werewolf

The gruesome creature here is a werewolf. According to legend, some people become wolves at times. Do you think this is likely to be true?

Susan first sketched a stick man, and then made him bend over slightly as she drew in his limbs and rounded his body. She looked for pictures of wolves to copy so that finally she could give him the head of a snarling beast. Look how hairy she has made the body and how long the nails on the hands and feet are. The teeth look really nasty, too, don't they?

Opposite are six animal heads that you can copy onto any drawing of a man or woman's body to make a really terrifying creature.

A devil

The horrible, evil-eyed, long-nosed, bald devil opposite is carrying a three-pronged spear known as a trident. He has a man's body but the legs and horns of a goat, as well as a long tail. The sketches show you how to put the drawing together in step-by-step stages. You might also like to draw in some background to your picture after you have finished the figure. Doesn't he look wicked! I'm glad he isn't looking this way!

This is an ink, water, and brush drawing. Graham made the swirls around the devil by trailing inky water over a very damp sheet of paper. This gives the effect of smoke.

A troll

Trolls play a large part in Scandinavian folk tales. They are very ugly but friendly dwarfs who play all sorts of jokes on human beings.

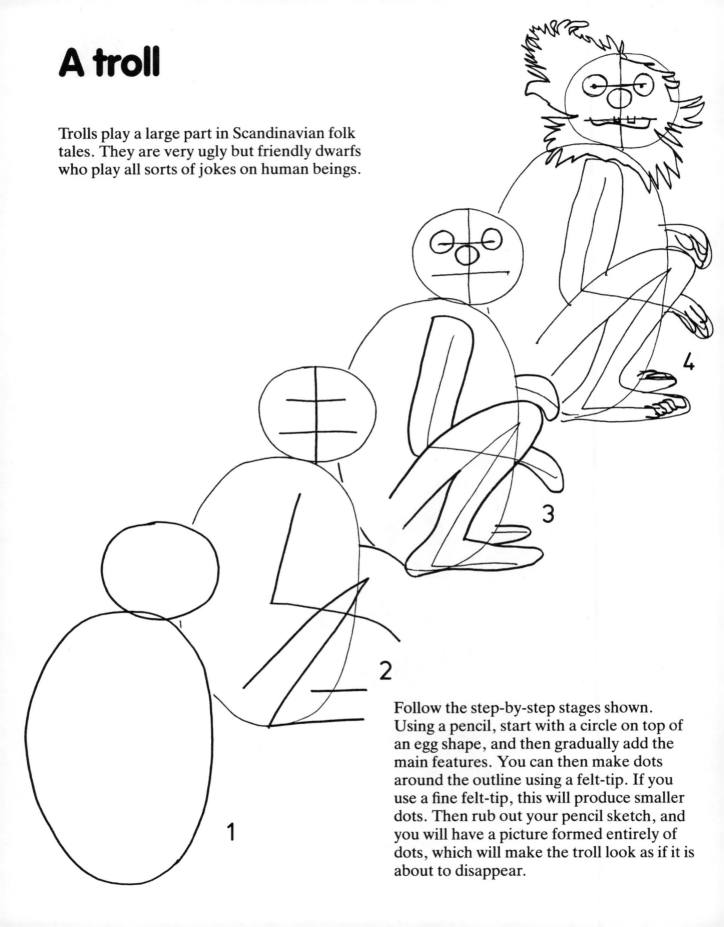

Follow the step-by-step stages shown. Using a pencil, start with a circle on top of an egg shape, and then gradually add the main features. You can then make dots around the outline using a felt-tip. If you use a fine felt-tip, this will produce smaller dots. Then rub out your pencil sketch, and you will have a picture formed entirely of dots, which will make the troll look as if it is about to disappear.

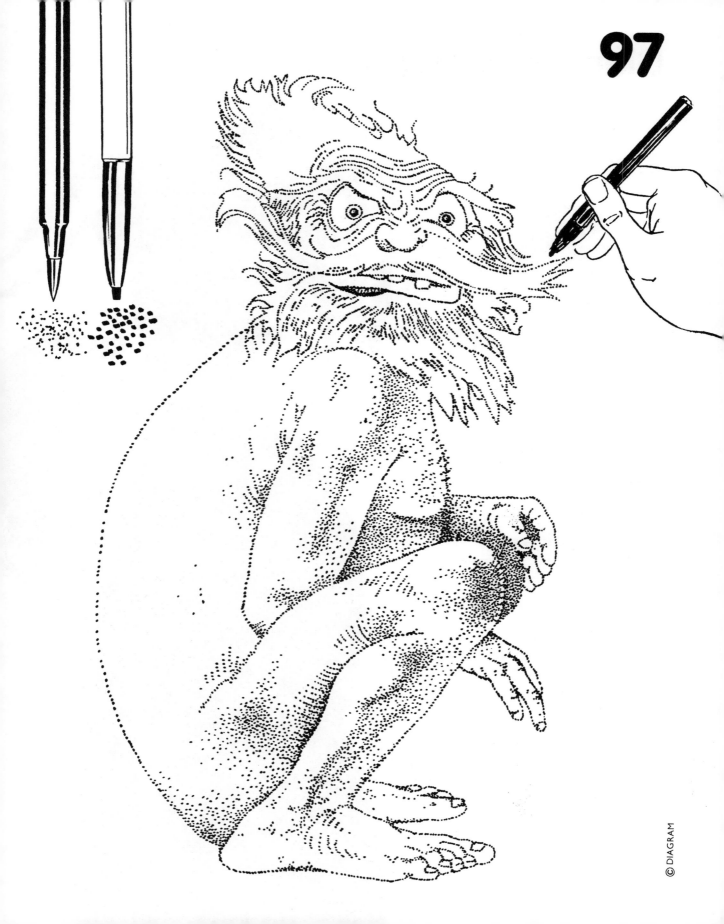

Giants and dwarfs

Giants are normal in size to other giants, but to us they would be enormous. Dwarfs, in fairy tales, however, would think *we* are enormous.

Any figure can be made to look like a giant simply by putting smaller figures or a very small object alongside him in your picture. You can also make a dwarf look tiny by making him far smaller than an object like a chair or a table, for instance.

Here is a giant reaching out to grab you!

To make giants huge draw them so big they burst out of the picture area.

Create your own giants and dwarfs by drawing tiny men beside huge figures. (Just look at the enormous fantasy figure on the left and the minute figures by his feet.

© DIAGRAM

Kali

This Indian goddess is a very terrifying figure and is often shown with a really ugly face, a necklace of human heads, a belt of human hands and a protruding blood-stained tongue. Notice her four arms: one is holding an axe; one holds a head; one holds a bowl; and the fourth is empty.

Follow the step-by-step sketches. Then add texture to the background by rubbing a wax crayon over a rough surface. Be sure to put in all her bangles, worn on the wrists, ankles and upper arms, and also add her earrings and headdress.

1

2

3

4

5

Microscopic monsters

I am sure you are not scared of tiny creatures that can only be seen under the microscope. But some of them have such odd shapes that, if they were bigger than you are, you might find them terrifying, even if they were quite friendly.

The one shown here has long branch-like arms and has been drawn in two different ways on this page – in ink, and in felt-tip with a little water added afterwards, using a brush.

Anna first sketched the picture opposite in pencil on thick, dark paper. She then used a fine brush to paint over the outline in white, and also added detail. She used a white pencil, too, to add some fine lines, and then dabbed on a little white paint with a sponge to make the dotted body.

You can make the blobs by blowing — not sucking! — through a straw at the paint while it is still wet. (But don't swallow any!)

©DIAGRAM

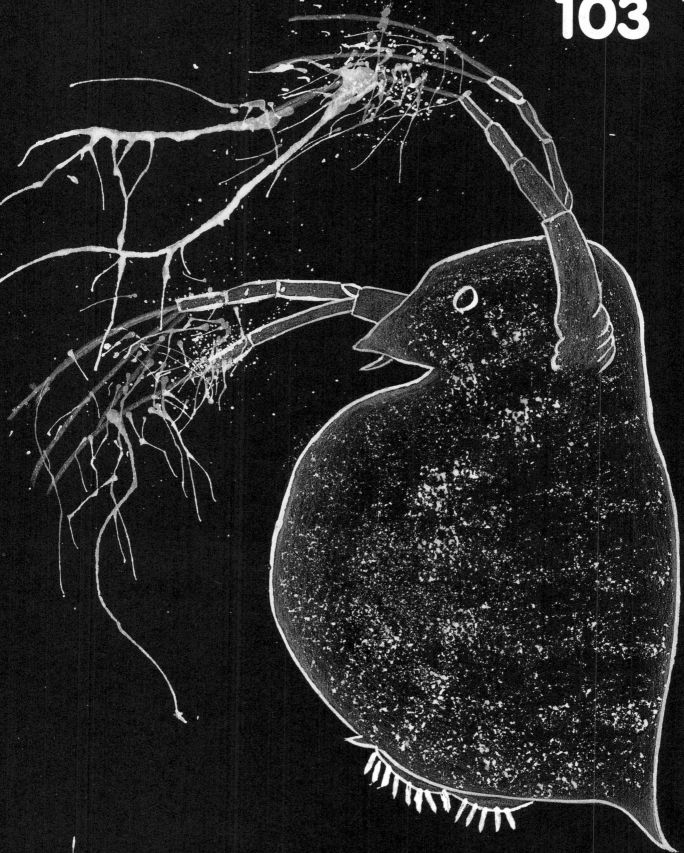

A Chinese dragon

This magnificent flying creature plays an important part in Chinese mythology and symbolizes wealth and power. The Chinese also say that if you were born in the Year of the Dragon (between 31st January 1976 and 17th February 1977), you are a Dragon-child and have particularly good imagination. You will also have a very lucky year, so they say, in the year 2000, which is also a Dragon year.

You might like to trace this drawing, using the technique described on pages 42–43. Notice the forked tongue, beard and four-clawed toes. You can find pictures of other wonderful dragons elsewhere in this book. Look at the index at the back of the book.

The sphinx

The sphinx is an Egyptian mythological monster with a human head and a lion's body. There are many stories about it. One concerns a riddle which the sphinx asked. What, it said, has two, three and four feet? Can you guess the answer? It is printed upside down at the bottom of this page.

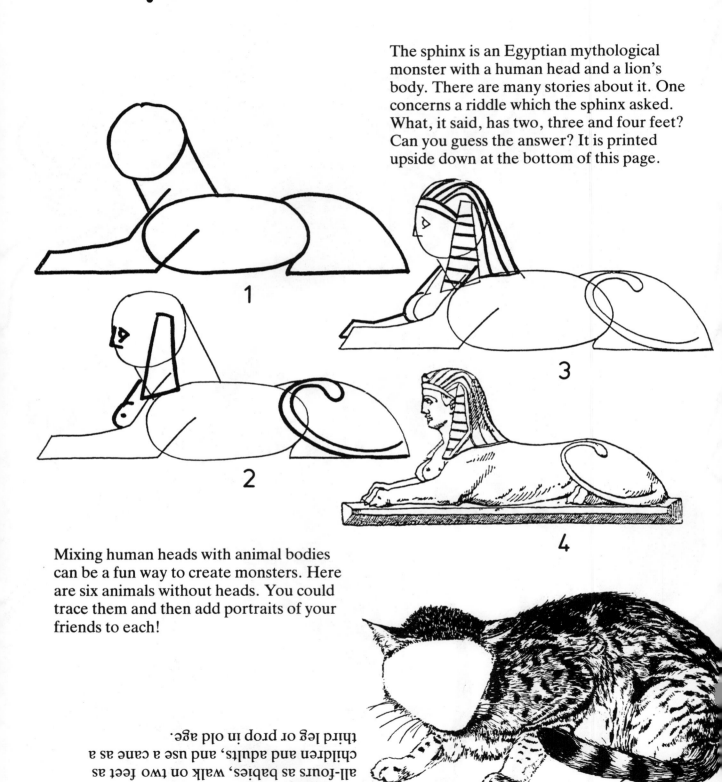

1

2

3

4

Mixing human heads with animal bodies can be a fun way to create monsters. Here are six animals without heads. You could trace them and then add portraits of your friends to each!

Answer: a human being – we crawl on all-fours as babies, walk on two feet as children and adults, and use a cane as a third leg or prop in old age.

A mermaid

This sea creature – half woman and half fish – is the subject of many legends and is said to tempt sailors with her beauty.

You could trace or copy this water-colour drawing by Graham. Give the mermaid long seaweed-like hair, a shell necklace, and perhaps webbed hands. Add scales to her tail by making criss-cross lines. Perhaps add background to your drawing and seat the mermaid on a rock or a sandy beach.

1

2

3

4

A centaur

The centaur is a mythical beast, half man and half horse. It is said to have been very warlike.

Follow the step-by-step sketches carefully, working in pencil, crayon or chalks, or trace the outline opposite.

You could also have fun making a whole book of half-and-half creatures. First make about ten drawings of various different monsters, each on a separate sheet of stiff paper of the same size. Then put the drawings one on top of the other, place them between two pieces of cardboard to make a cover, and staple them together at the left-hand edge. Now open the covers and cut each page in half horizontally. You can then flip over the top or bottom halves and create all sorts of crazy monsters.

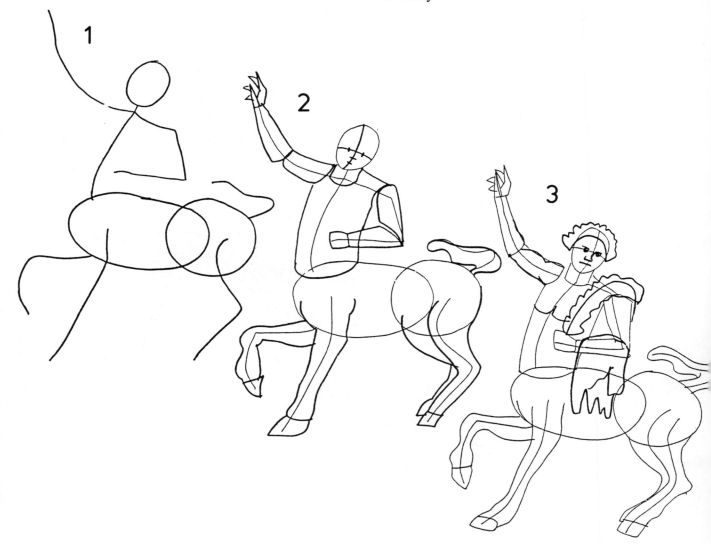

The abominable snowman

People have been hunting in the Himalayas for the abominable snowman (or yeti, as it is also known) for hundreds of years. His huge footprints have been seen, but no one knows for sure that he exists.

James drew a pencil outline of what he thought the yeti might look like, using a piece of white paper. Then he cut it out and stuck it onto black cardboard. Next he used white and brown chalks to mark in the shaggy fur and facial details. You could also flick some white paint onto the black cardboard using an old toothbrush to create the effect of a blizzard, but don't make too much mess!

©DIAGRAM

A mud man

Just imagine a creature made entirely of mud! Every time this monster went out in the rain, he would get terribly slimy and completely misshapen. Ugh! How disgusting!

You can start to draw him with simple circles and oval shapes. Gradually add more detail and give lots of wriggles to the outline. Paul shaded in parts of the body with a soft 2B pencil, but he also tried using dots (as you can see in the smaller drawing opposite) to get a different effect. You could choose either of these methods.

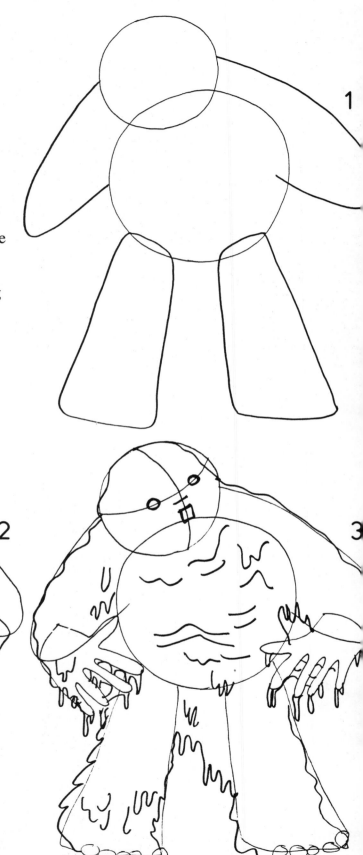

Twenty thousand leagues under the sea

This is the title of a famous book by Jules Verne. It can be fun to imagine all the different sorts of creatures that might exist in the depths of the ocean, where no one has ever been.

Here are two which are really quite frightening. I shouldn't like to meet them next time I go snorkling! Both have a human-like form. You could copy or trace them.

Then turn your drawing into a monster by adding flipper feet, tentacles, scales and claws. Who knows what might be lurking at the bottom of the deepest seas!

King Kong

This giant gorilla is the subject of an old and very popular adventure film that is repeated every now and then on TV. As you can see from the woman he is holding in his hand, he was many times the size of a human. In the film, he lives in the United States and, since he is larger than all the buildings, terrorizes everyone.

Graham used ink and a brush for this drawing. Follow the step-by-step sketches carefully, or trace the outline and then add details. Don't forget to make him snarl!

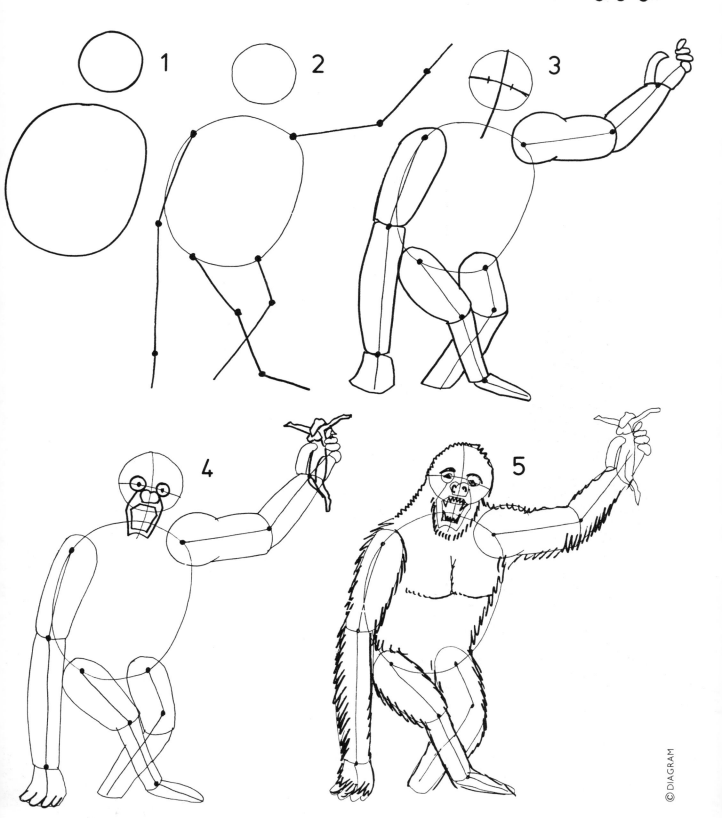

1

2

3

4

5

Godzilla

1

2

3

4

First featured in a Japanese film, Godzilla is
a gigantic fantasy creature with spines all
the way down his back and fiery, radioactive
breath. Those are not toy trains he is
holding but real railway carriages! (Doesn't
he remind you of a dinosaur?)

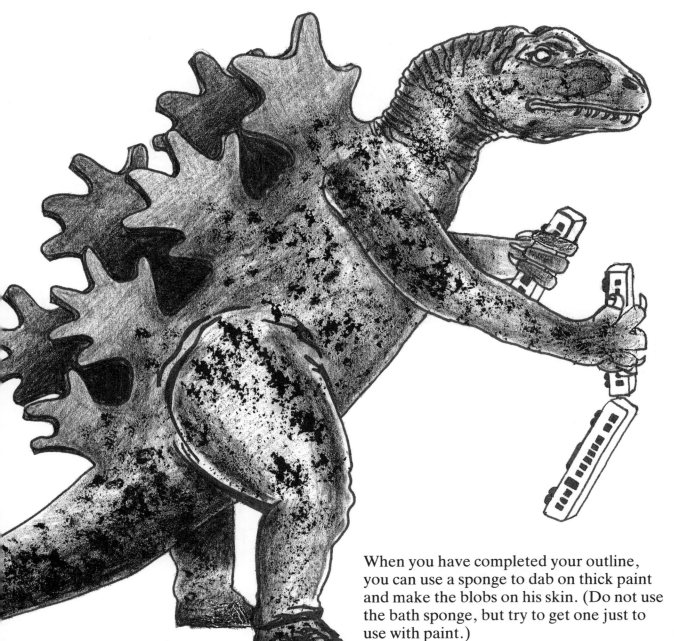

When you have completed your outline,
you can use a sponge to dab on thick paint
and make the blobs on his skin. (Do not use
the bath sponge, but try to get one just to
use with paint.)

©DIAGRAM

A harpy

1

2

3

Have fun drawing creatures that have human bodies and animal heads, or vice versa, like those opposite.

The strange winged creature on this page, with the head of a woman, is found in several Greek myths and is said to emerge from the wind and carry off both people and objects. She is a harpy.

Start by drawing a circle for the head, an oval for the body, and a skirt-shape at the bottom, as shown. Then add the upstretched arms, breasts and claws, and next the hair and wings. Her fingers, notice, are bent to look like claws and have long, pointed nails.

4

5

©DIAGRAM

A golem

This gigantic creature comes from an Eastern European Jewish folktale. The golem was made from clay, but then came to life by magic.

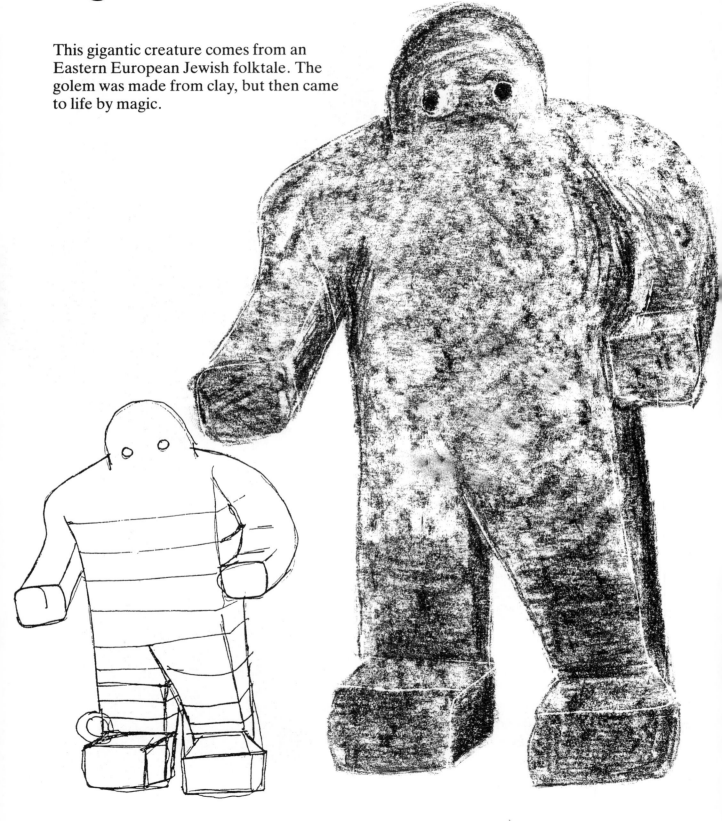

Mary drew him in chalk and also in wax crayon, within a pencil outline. Which do you prefer? Look how much bigger the golem is than the man who is running away from him, terrified by his size and the fact that he has come to life so mysteriously!

This drawing was shaded by placing thin tracing paper over a rough surface and rubbing with a wax crayon. Above is a strip that shows the darker effect you get if you press harder with the crayon.

©DIAGRAM

The cyclops

This one-eyed, man-eating cyclops might enjoy you for breakfast! He appears in an ancient Greek story called the Odyssey. A man called Odysseus outwits him and then blinds him by poking a stick in his single eye.

Start with a stick creature, as shown, and develop your drawing in stages. To get the fluffy legs, use a crayon but keep to pencil for the rest of the picture. The step-by-step sketches on page 70–71 will help you to draw the head. Watch out! I think he is about to attack!

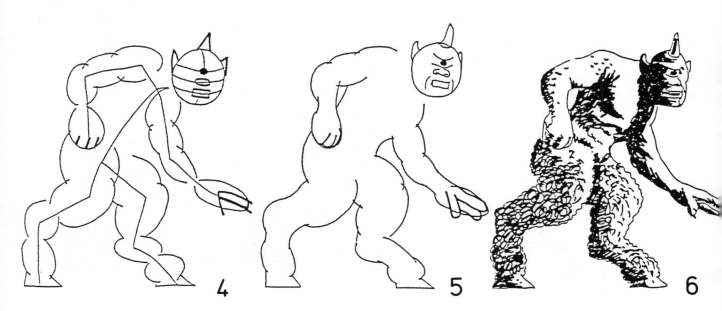

Ghosts and ghouls

Some people would say that ghosts and ghouls (or spirits) are the most frightening monsters of all. Their outlines are certainly easy to draw.

You can get great effects by sketching ghosts in white chalks over darker backgrounds.

Some paints and inks are soluble. This means that they will dissolve in water. If you use soluble paints, you will find that they do not cover marks that have been made with wax crayons. There are some very exciting special effects you can get in this way, too.

White chalk on dark paper also gives a scary look, especially if you have drawn furniture that can be seen through the ghost.

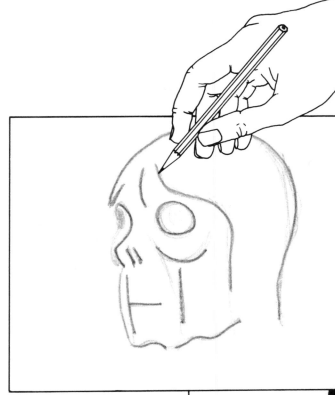

1

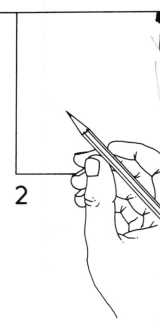

2

When you draw ghosts, try to give them lots of different expressions, like those below.

1 First plan your drawing using a soft pencil. Remember to work on strong paper because you will be adding a water-based paint or ink later.

2 Next, put in the detail and dark areas with a hard pencil, ballpoint, brush or felt-tip.

3 Now rub a white, pink or pale brown wax crayon over those areas you would like to keep light in your drawing.

4 Paint over the dark tones in your drawing. Then try to paint over the areas covered with wax crayon. You should find that they do not take the paint. The result is that there will be areas in your picture that have different textures.

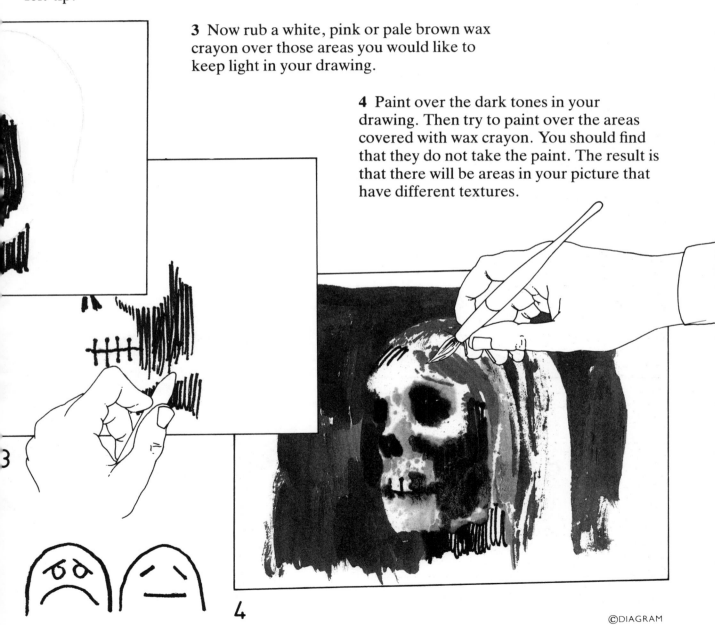

An octopus

Copy these squiggles, each on a separate
piece of paper but of course much larger.
Then have fun turning them into monsters,
perhaps even weirder in shape than the
octopus opposite.

More monsters of the deep

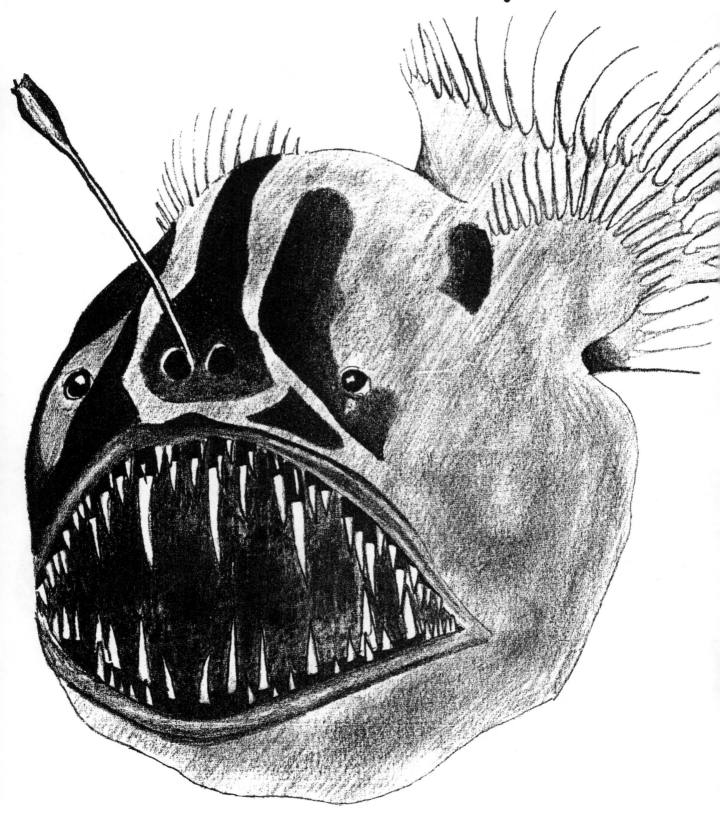

This is an angler fish that lives deep in the sea. It is a real creature, not a fantasy one. To very much smaller fish, it is, of course, like a monster, although it is nowhere near as big as a whale. It uses its top fin like a fishing rod. The end of it is fluorescent and shines in the dark, attracting small sea creatures which the angler fish then catches in its fearsome jaws.

Start with a simple circle and then develop the drawing as shown.

As always, a soft (B grade) pencil is best for shading, and a hard (H grade) pencil is best for firm lines – the edges of all those pointed teeth, for instance. Remember to keep your pencils well sharpened so that they are ready for use. Wax crayons are even better for shading large areas.

1

2

3

4

This is a hammerhead shark. It has eyes that stick out from the hammerheads on the sides of its head. Try to copy it at a much larger size.

©DIAGRAM

Bats

Most bats are harmless, but some can look quite scary. Just look at the face on the left! or at the bottom right-hand corner of the page opposite.

You can trace the three bats opposite and then enlarge them using the method described on pages 48–49. You might then like to make a small hole in each and hang them up with knotted string, as shown. Someone is in for a rather nasty shock when he wakes up!

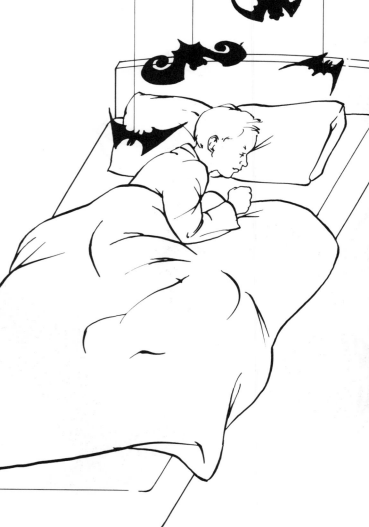

You could also make a large bat by folding over a sheet of thick paper, drawing half a bat and cutting it out. Then draw in the details of its wings and body.

Space aliens

If aliens were to land here from outer space, or if we found creatures on another planet, what do you think they might look like?

They might or might not wear clothes. They might have faces like ours, or have an eye at the back of the head. Their sight might be as powerful as a telescope, and they might be able to run at a tremendous speed.

The adult and baby aliens opposite were drawn by Andrew. You would not call them handsome, would you?

You can trace them, and then make up some space monsters of your own. Their faces would make excellent masks.

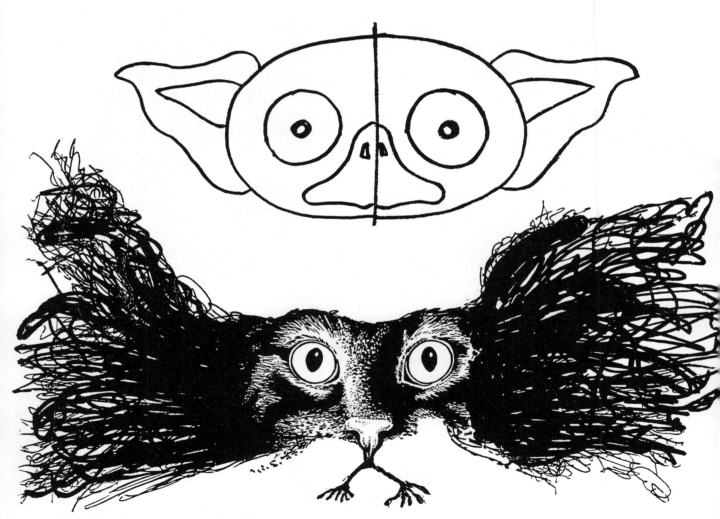

Perhaps give your creatures from outer space special names. I have called this one a pussiejumble.

©DIAGRAM

Metal monsters

Robots are fun: but if you let your imagination run riot, they could turn into monsters that might attack and even destroy their makers.

Here are some simple objects from which you can construct your own monster.

Take a look at the robot monster shown here. Then design some of your own, making them look as wicked as you can, with ray gun, laser and radar attachments and perhaps hands like giant pincers that could crush a human being. You might also include a very much smaller person in your picture so that it really seems that the robot is so huge that it can easily take over everyone.

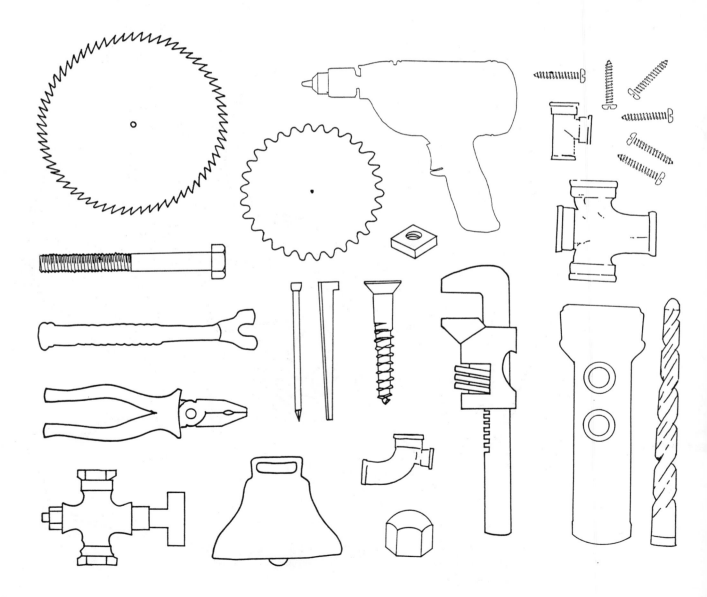

This is robot iiii, known as four eyes (four letter i's), and his dog Roller. I made it by cutting up pictures of tools, sticking them together and then drawing in extra parts.

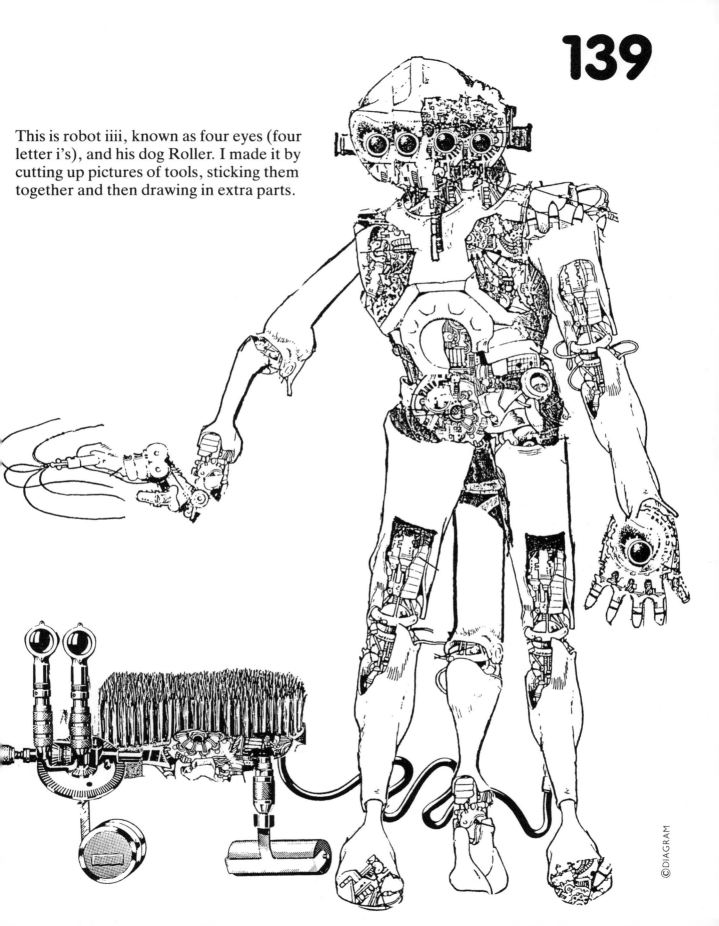

These squares can
be used for enlarging
or reducing your drawings,
as described on pages
48–49.

Index

Here and at the front of the book are details
from some of the drawings featured. Can
you find the pages on which they appear?